'Charlie Fox. In small bites. With sharp teeth.'
This is a revamped and extended edition of the Fox Five
collection of short stories by the highly acclaimed crime thriller
writer, Zoë Sharp. It includes the original five stories, plus
another four, available in one volume for the first time. All these
tales feature ex-Special Forces soldier turned self-defence expert
and bodyguard, **Charlotte 'Charlie' Fox**.

A Bridge Too Far
Postcards From Another Country
Served Cold*
Off Duty
Truth And Lies
Across The Broken Line
Kill Me Again Slowly
Risk Assessment
Hounded

*Nominated for the Crime Writers' Association (CWA) UK Short
Story Dagger Award

Zoë Sharp's short stories have appeared in Ellery Queen Mystery
Magazine and Strand Magazine, as well as award-winning
anthologies in the UK and USA. They have been used in school
textbooks, turned into short films, included in many Best Of
collections, and nominated twice for the Crime Writers'
Association (CWA) Short Story Dagger.

"I highly recommend this series!"

— BESTSELLING AUTHOR, IAN RANKIN

"Male and female crime fiction readers alike will find Sharp's writing style addictively readable."

— PAUL GOAT ALLEN, *CHICAGO TRIBUNE*

"Scarily good."

— BESTSELLING AUTHOR, LEE CHILD

"Whenever I turn the first page on a Charlie Fox novel, I know that her creator is going to serve up a complex, fast-paced military-grade action romp than can hold its head high in the male-dominated thriller world."

— LINDA WILSON, *CRIME REVIEW UK*

"Zoë Sharp is one of the sharpest, coolest, and most intriguing writers I know. She delivers dramatic, action-packed novels with characters we really care about."

— BESTSELLING AUTHOR, HARLAN COBEN

"This is hard-edged fiction at its best."

— MICHELE LEBER, *BOOKLIST* STARRED REVIEW FOR
FIFTH VICTIM

"Superb."

— KEN BRUEN, BESTSELLING AUTHOR OF THE JACK
TAYLOR SERIES, **THE GUARDS, BLITZ**

"If you don't like Zoë Sharp there's something wrong with you. Go and live in a cave and get the hell out of my gene pool! There are few writers who go right to the top of my TBR pile—Zoë Sharp is one of them."

— STUART MACBRIDE, BESTSELLING AUTHOR OF THE
LOGAN MCRAE SERIES

"Every book in this suspenseful series opens with a scene that grabs the reader by the throat and doesn't let go until the final page… Sharp creates some of the best action sequences in fiction… Don't miss out on one of the best thriller writers around."

— TED HERTEL JR, *DEADLY PLEASURES MYSTERY MAGAZINE*

"The bloody bar fights are bloody brilliant, and Charlie's skills are formidable and for real."

— MARILYN STASIO, *NEW YORK TIMES*, ON **KILLER INSTINCT**

"What I love about this series is the fact that Zoë Sharp pulls the reader into every scenario—creates a world where you are part of the action and then leaves you gasping for breath as the final conclusion comes around. It's a total experience and one I look forward to each and every time!"

— NOELLE HOLTEN, *CRIME BOOK JUNKIE*

"Charlotte 'Charlie' Fox is one of the most vivid and engaging heroines ever to swagger onto the pages of a book. Where Charlie goes, thrills follow."

— BESTSELLING AUTHOR, TESS GERRITSEN, AUTHOR OF
THE RIZZOLI & ISLES SERIES

for Martin Edwards
who persuaded me to write my first
Charlie Fox short story

FOX FIVE RELOADED

CHARLIE FOX SHORT STORY COLLECTION

ZOË SHARP

CONTENTS

ALSO BY ZOË SHARP

THE LAST TIME SHE DIED

For Behind the Scenes, Bonus Features, Freebies, Sneak Peeks and
advance notice of new releases, sign up for Zoë's **VIP list** at
www.ZoeSharp.com/vip-mailing-list.

AUTHOR'S NOTE

INTRODUCTION

Meet **Charlotte 'Charlie' Fox**—ex-Special Forces soldier turned self-defence expert and bodyguard—protagonist of Zoë Sharp's award-winning, highly acclaimed crime thriller series.

"Ill-tempered, aggressive and borderline psychotic, Fox is also compassionate, introspective and highly principled: arguably one of the most enigmatic—and coolest—heroines in contemporary genre fiction." **Paul Goat Allen, Chicago Tribune**

In **A Bridge Too Far**, we meet Charlie Fox before she's become a professional in the world of close protection. When she agrees to hang out with the local Dangerous Sports Club, she has no idea how soon it will live up to its name.

Postcards From Another Country has Charlie Fox guarding the ultra-rich Dempsey family against attempted assassination—no matter where the danger lies.

A finalist for the CWA Short Story Dagger, **Served Cold** puts another tough woman centre stage—the mysterious Layla, with betrayal in her past and murder in her heart.

Off Duty finds Charlie Fox taking time away from close protection after injury. She still finds trouble, even in an out-of-season health spa in the Catskill Mountains.

A longer story than the others, **Truth And Lies** puts all Charlie Fox's skills and ingenuity to the test as she has to single-handedly extract a news team from a rapidly escalating war zone.

And now, for Fox Five Reloaded, there are another FOUR Charlie Fox stories included.

In **Across The Broken Line**, we follow Charlie Fox through a fragmented timescale of cross and double-cross as she fights to keep her principal alive—whoever that might turn out to be.

Taking on the bad guys is hard enough for Charlie Fox in the real world, never mind in the alternate reality of **Kill Me Again Slowly**, where literally *anything* could happen. (Originally included in the Anthony Award-winning anthology, Murder Under The Oaks.)

In **Risk Assessment**, a serial killer's method of selecting his victims is immaculately conceived and carried out with ruthless precision and seemingly nothing left to chance. But sometimes even the most carefully thought-out plans can go awry.

And finally, **Hounded** is my take on the Sir Arthur Conan Doyle classic, Hound Of The Baskervilles. This was originally written for the anthology For The Sake Of The Game, short stories inspired by the Sherlock Holmes' canon. My version brings Holmes into modern day and into contact with Charlie Fox. But Charlie isn't staying on the moors hunting the infamous hound. She has altogether different prey in mind…

A BRIDGE TOO FAR

THIS WAS the very first short story I ever wrote featuring Charlie Fox.

The story is set at roughly the same point in her life as the opening book in the series, KILLER INSTINCT, when Charlie is living in Lancashire in the UK and making a living teaching self-defence to local women.

She has been out of the Army for several years by this time, but has not yet plunged into a new career in close protection. Such a possibility is a long way from her mind, even though she already demonstrates the cool-headedness in a crisis that makes her so well suited for the job.

A Bridge Too Far came about because I was invited to submit a story for the UK Crime Writers' Association short story anthology, GREEN FOR DANGER: CRIMES IN THE COUNTRY, by the editor, Martin Edwards. (I did not tell him that I had never attempted a short story before until after he had accepted it for publication.) But as soon as Martin mentioned the requirement of a rural setting, a true story sprang to mind.

Some years ago a friend told me about being a member of a local Dangerous Sports Club. Bicycle abseiling was one of their pursuits, if I remember right—and yes, that is just as crazy as it sounds.

Bridge swinging was another speciality, which did indeed take place from an old disused railway viaduct that stretched across a farmer's field. And the farmer did indeed object to their activities for exactly the reason stated in this story.

But after that, all bets were off and I let my imagination take hold.

As well as the original CWA anthology, A Bridge Too Far also appeared in Ellery Queen Mystery Magazine.

————

I WATCHED with a kind of horrified fascination as the boy climbed onto the narrow parapet. Below his feet, the elongated brick arches of the old viaduct stretched, so I'd been told, exactly one hundred and twenty-three feet to the ground. He balanced on the crumbling brickwork at the edge, casual and unconcerned.

My God, I thought, *He's going to do it. He's actually going to jump.*

"Don't prat around, Adam," one of the others said. I was still sorting out their names. Paul, that was it. He was a medical student, tall and bony with a long almost roman nose. "If you're going to do it, do it, or let someone else have their turn."

"Now now," Adam said, wagging a finger. "Don't be bitchy."

Paul glared at him, took a step forwards, but the cool blonde-haired girl, Diana, put a hand on his arm.

"Leave him alone, Paul," Diana said, and there was a faint snap to her voice. She'd been introduced as Adam's girlfriend, so I suppose she had the right to be protective. "He'll jump when he's ready. You'll have your chance to impress the newbies."

She flicked unfriendly eyes in my direction as she spoke but I didn't rise to it. Heights didn't draw or repel me the way I knew they did with most people but that didn't mean I was inclined to throw myself off a bridge to prove my courage. I'd already done that at enough other times, in enough other places.

Beside me, my friend Sam muttered under his breath, "OK, I'm impressed. No way are you getting me up there."

I grinned at him. It was Sam who'd told me about the local Dangerous Sports Club who trekked out to this disused viaduct in the middle of nowhere. There they tied one end of a rope to the far parapet and brought the other end up underneath between the supports before tying it round their ankles.

And then they jumped.

The idea, as Sam explained it, was to propel yourself

outwards as though diving off a cliff and trying to avoid the rocks below. I suspected this wasn't an analogy with resonance for either of us, but the technique ensured that when you reached the end of your tether, so to speak, the slack was taken up progressively and you swung backwards and forwards under the bridge in a graceful arc.

Jump straight down, however, and you would be jerked to a stop hard enough to break your spine. They used modern climbing rope with a fair amount of give in it but it was far from the elastic gear required by the bungee jumper. That was for wimps.

Sam knew the group's leader, Adam Lane, from the nearby university, where Sam was something incomprehensible to do with computers and Adam was the star of the track and field teams. He was one of these magnetic golden boys who breezed effortlessly through life, always looking for a greater challenge, something to set their heartbeat racing. And for Adam the unlikely pastime of bridge swinging, it seemed, was it.

I hadn't believed Sam's description of the activity and had made the mistake of expressing my scepticism out loud. So, here I was on a bright but surprisingly nippy Sunday morning in May, waiting for the first of these lunatics to launch himself into the abyss.

Now, though, Adam put his hands on his hips and breathed in deep, looking around with a certain intensity at the landscape. His stance, up there on the edge of the precipice, was almost a pose.

We were halfway across the valley floor, in splendid isolation. The tracks to this Brunel masterpiece had been long since ripped up and carted away. The only clue to their existence was the footpath that led across the fields from the lay-by on the road where Sam and I had left our motorbikes. The other cars there, I guessed, belonged to Adam and his friends.

The view from the viaduct was stunning, the sides of the valley curving away at either side as though seen through a fish-eye lens. It was still early, so that the last of the dawn mist clung to the dips and hollows, and it was quiet enough to hear the world turning.

"Hello there! Not starting without us, are you?" called a girl's cheery voice, putting a scatter of crows to flight, breaking the spell. A flash of annoyance passed across Adam's handsome features.

A young couple was approaching. Like the other three DSC members, they were wearing high-tech outdoor clothing—lightweight trousers you can wash and dry in thirty seconds, and lairy-coloured fleeces.

The boy was short and muscular, a look emphasised by the fact he'd turned his coat collar up against the chill, giving him no neck to speak of. He tramped onto the bridge and almost threw his rucksack down with the others.

"What's the matter, Michael?" Adam said, his voice a lazy taunt. "Get out of bed on the wrong side?"

The newcomer gave him a single, vicious look and said nothing.

The girl was shorter and plumper than Diana. Her gaze flicked nervously from one to the other, latching onto the rope already secured round Adam's legs as if glad of the distraction. "Oh *Adam*, you're never jumping today are you?" she cried. "I didn't think you were supposed to—"

"I'm perfectly OK, Izzy darling," Adam drawled. His eyes shifted meaningfully towards Sam and me, then back again.

Izzy opened her mouth to speak, closing it again with a snap as she caught on. Her pale complexion bloomed into sudden pink across her cheekbones and she bent to fuss with her own rucksack. She drew out a stainless steel flask and held it up like an offering. "I brought coffee."

"How very thoughtful of you, Izzy dear," Diana said, speaking down her well-bred nose at the other girl. "You always were so very accommodating."

Izzy's colour deepened. "I'm not sure there's enough for everybody," she went on, dogged. She nodded apologetically to us. "No-one told me there'd be new people coming. I'm Izzy, by the way."

"Sam Pickering," Sam put in, "and this is Charlie Fox."

Izzy smiled a little shyly, then a sudden thought struck her. "You're not thinking of joining are you?" she said in an anxious tone. "Only, it's not certain we're going to carry on with the club for much longer."

"'Course we are," Michael said brusquely, raising his dark stubbled chin out of his collar for the first time. "Just because Adam has to give up, no reason for the rest of us to pack it in. We'll manage without him."

The others seemed to hold their breath while they checked Adam's response to this dismissive declaration, but he seemed to have lost interest in the squabbles of lesser mortals. He continued to stand on the parapet, untroubled by the yawning drop below him, staring into the middle distance like an ocean sailor.

"That's not the only reason we might have to stop," the tall bony boy, Paul said. "In fact, here comes another right now."

He nodded across the far side of the field. We all turned and I noticed for the first time that a man on a red Honda quad bike was making a beeline for us across the dewy grass.

"Oh shit," Michael muttered. "Wacko Jacko. That's all we need."

"Who is he?" Sam asked, watching the purposeful way the quad was bearing down on us.

"He's the local farmer," Paul explained. "He owns all the land round here and he's dead against us using the viaduct, but it's a public right of way and legally he can't stop us. That doesn't stop the old bugger coming and giving us a hard time every Sunday."

"Mr Jackson's a strict Methodist you see," Izzy said quietly as the quad drew nearer. "It's not trespassing that's the problem—it's the fact that when the boys jump, well, they do tend to swear a bit. I think he objects to the blasphemy."

I eyed the farmer warily as he finally braked to a halt at the edge of the bridge and cut the quad's engine. The main reason for my caution was the elderly double-barrelled Baikal shotgun he lifted out of the rack on one side and brought with him.

Jackson came stumping along the bridge towards us with the kind of rolling, twitching gait that denotes a pair of totally worn-out knees. He wore a flat cap with tar on the peak and a tatty raincoat tied together with orange bailer twine. As he closed on us he snapped the Baikal shut, and I instinctively edged myself slightly in front of Sam.

"'Morning Mr Jackson," Izzy called, the tension sending her voice into a high waver.

The farmer ignored the greeting, his eyes fixed on Adam. It was only when Michael and Paul physically blocked his path that he seemed to notice the rest of us.

"I've told you lot before. You've no right to do this on my land," he said gruffly, clutching the shotgun almost nervously, as though suddenly aware he was outnumbered. "You been warned."

"And you've been told that *you* have no right to stop us, you daft old bugger," Adam said, the derision clear in his voice.

Jackson's ruddy face congested. He tried to push closer to Adam, but Paul caught the lapel of his raincoat and shoved him backwards. With a fraction less aggression the whole thing could have passed off with a few harsh words but after this, there was only one way it was going to go.

The scuffle was brief. Jackson was hard and fit from years of manual labour but the boys both had thirty years on him. It was the shotgun that worried me the most. Michael had grabbed hold of the barrel and was trying to wrench it from the farmer's grasp, while *he* was determined to keep hold of it. The business end of the Baikal swung wildly across the rest of us.

Izzy was shrieking, ducked down with her hands over her ears. I piled Sam backwards, starting to head for the end of the bridge.

The blast of the shotgun discharging stopped my breath. I flinched at the pellets twanging off the brickwork as the shot spread. The echo rolled away up and down the valley like a call to battle.

The silence that followed was quickly broken by Izzy's whimpering cries. She was still on the ground, staring in horrified disbelief at the blood seeping through a couple of small holes in the leg of her trousers.

Paul crouched near to her, hands fluttering over the wounds without actually wanting to touch them. Sam had turned vaguely green at the first sign of blood, but he unwound the cotton scarf from under the neck of his leathers and handed it over to me without a word. I moved Paul aside quietly and padded the makeshift dressing onto Izzy's leg.

"It's only a couple of pellets," I told her. "It's not serious. Hold this against it as hard as you can. You'll be fine."

Michael had managed to wrestle the Baikal away from Jackson. He turned and took in Izzy's state, then pointed the shotgun meaningfully back at the shaken farmer, settling his finger onto the second trigger.

"You bastard," he ground out.

"Michael, stop it," Diana said.

Michael ignored her, his dark eyes fixed menacingly on Jackson. "You've just shot my girlfriend."

"*Michael!*" Diana tried again, shouting this time. She had quite a voice for one so slender. "Stop it! Don't you understand? *Where's Adam?*"

We all turned then, looked back to the section of parapet where he'd been standing. The lichen-covered wall was peppered with tiny fresh chips but the parapet itself was empty.

Adam was gone.

I ran to the edge and leaned out over it as far as I dared. A hundred and twenty-three feet below me, a crumpled form lay utterly still on the grassy slope. The blood was a bright halo around his head.

"Adam!" Diana yelled, her voice cracking. "Oh, God. Can you hear me?"

I stepped back, caught Sam's enquiring glance and shook my head.

Paul was already hurrying towards the end of the bridge to pick his way down beneath the arches. I went after him, snagged his arm as he started his descent.

"I'll go," I said. When he looked at me dubiously, I added, "I know First-Aid if there's anything to be done and if not, well"—I shrugged—"I've seen dead bodies before."

His face was grave for a moment, then he nodded. "What can we do?"

"Get an ambulance—Izzy probably needs one even if Adam doesn't—and call the police." He nodded again and had already started back up the slope when I added, "Oh, and try not to let Michael shoot that bloody farmer."

"Why not?" Paul demanded bitterly. "He deserves it." And then he was gone.

It was a relatively easy path down to where Adam's body lay. Close to, it wasn't particularly pretty. I hardly needed to search for a pulse at his outflung wrist to know the boy was dead. Still, the relatively soft surface had kept him largely intact, enough for me to tell that it wasn't any shotgun blast that had killed him. Gravity had done that all by itself.

I took off my jacket and gently laid it over the top half of the body, covering his head. It was the only thing I could do for him, and even that was more to protect the sensibilities of the living.

When I looked up I could see half of the rope dangling from the opposite side of the bridge high above my head, its loose end swaying gently. The other end was still tied around Adam's ankles. It had snapped during his fall, but why?

Had Jackson's shot severed the rope at the moment when Adam had either lost his balance and fallen, or as he'd chosen to jump?

I got to my feet and followed the rope along the ground to where the severed end lay coiled in the grass. I used a twig to carefully lift it up enough to examine it.

And then I knew.

The embankment seemed a hell of a lot steeper on the way up than it had on the way down. I ran all the way and was totally out of breath by the time I regained the bridge. But I was just in time.

Diana was crouched next to Izzy, holding her hand. Paul and Sam were standing a few feet behind Michael, eyeing him with varying amounts of fear and mistrust. The thickset youth had the shotgun wedged up under Jackson's chin, using it to force his upper body backwards over the top of the parapet. Michael's face was blenched with anger, teetering on the edge of control.

"He's dead, isn't he?" He didn't take his eyes off the farmer as I approached.

"Yes," I said carefully, "but Jackson didn't kill him, Michael."

"But he must have done." It was Paul who spoke. "We all saw—"

"You saw nothing," I cut in. "The gun went off and Adam either jumped or fell, but he wasn't shot. The rope gave out. That's why he's dead."

"That's ridiculous," Diana said, haughty rather than anguished. "The breaking strain on the ropes we use is enormous. No way could it have simply broken. The shot must have hit it."

"It didn't," I said. "It was cut halfway through. With a knife."

Even Michael reacted to that one, taking the shotgun away from Jackson's neck as he swivelled round to face me. I could see the indentations the barrels had left in the scrawny skin of the old man's throat.

Chances like that don't come very often. I took a quick step closer, looped my arm over the one of Michael's that held the gun and brought my elbow back sharply into the fleshy vee between his ribs.

He doubled over, gasping, letting go of the weapon. I picked it out of his hands and stepped back again. It was all over in a moment.

The others watched in silence as I broke the Baikal and picked out the remaining live cartridge. Once it was unloaded I put the gun down propped against the brickwork and dropped the cartridge into my pocket. Michael had caught his breath enough to think about coming at me, but it was Sam who intervened.

"I wouldn't if you know what's good for you," he said, his voice kindly. "Charlie's a bit of an expert at this type of thing. She'd eat you for breakfast."

Michael favoured me with a hard stare. I returned it flat and level. I don't know what he thought he saw but he backed off, sullen, rubbing his stomach.

"So," I said, "the question is, who cut Adam's rope?"

For a moment there was total silence. "Look, we either have this out now, or you get the third degree when the police arrive," I said, shrugging. "I assume you *did* call them?" I added in Paul's direction.

"No, but I did," Sam said, brandishing his mobile phone. "They're on their way. I've said I'll wait for them up on the road. Show them the way. Will you be OK down here?"

I nodded. "I'll cope," I said. "Oh and Sam—when they arrive, tell them it looks like murder."

Nobody spoke as Sam started out across the field. He eyed the quad bike with some envy as he passed, but went on foot.

"I still say the old bastard deserves shooting," Michael muttered.

"I didn't do nothing," Jackson blurted out suddenly. Relieved of the immediate threat to his life he simply stood looking dazed with his shoulders slumped. "I never would have fired. It was him who grabbed my hand! He's the one who forced my finger down on the trigger!"

He waved towards Michael, who flushed angrily at the charge. I replayed the scene again and recalled the way the stocky boy had been struggling with Jackson for control of the gun. It had looked for all the world like a genuine skirmish but it could just as easily have been a convenient set-up.

When no one immediately spoke up in his defence, Michael rounded on us.

"How can you believe anything so *stupid*?" he bit out. "Adam was a good mate. I would have given him my last cent."

"Didn't like sharing your girlfriend with him, though, did you?" Paul said quietly.

Izzy, still lying on the ground, gave an audible gasp. I checked to see how Diana was taking the news of her dead boyfriend's apparent infidelity but there was little to be gleaned from her cool and colourless expression.

A brief spasm of what might have been fear passed across Michael's face. "You can't believe I'd want to kill him for that?" he said and gave a harsh laugh. "Defending Izzy's honour? Come on! I knew right from the start that she's not exactly choosy."

Izzy had begun to cry. "He loved me," she managed between sobs, and it wasn't immediately clear if she was referring to Michael or Adam. "He told me he loved me."

Diana sat back, still looking at Izzy, but without really seeing her. "That's what he tells—told—all of them," she said, almost to herself. "Wanted to hear them say it back to him, I suppose." She smiled then, a little sadly. "Adam always did need to be adored. The centre of attention."

"You're just saying that but it wasn't true," Izzy cried. "He loved me. He was going to give you up but he wanted to let you down gently, not to hurt your feelings. He was just waiting for the right time."

"Oh Izzy, of course he wasn't going to give me up," Diana said, her tone one of great patience, as though talking to the very young, or the very slow. "He used to come straight from your bed back to mine and tell me all about it." She laughed, a high brittle peal. "How desperately keen you were. How eager to please."

"And you didn't *mind*?" I asked, fighting to keep the disbelief and the distaste buried.

"Of course not," Diana said, sounding vaguely surprised that I should feel the need to ask. She sighed. "Adam had some… interesting tastes. There were some things that I simply drew the line at, but Izzy"—her eyes slipped away from mine to skim dispassionately over the girl lying cringing in front of her —"well, she would do just about anything he asked. Pathetic, really."

"Are you really trying to tell me that you *knew* your boyfriend was sleeping around and you didn't care at all?"

Diana stood, looked down her nose again in that way she had. The way that indicated I was being too bourgeois for words. "Naturally," she said. "I understood Adam perfectly and I understood that this was his last fling at life while he still had the chance."

"What do you mean, while he still had the chance?" I said. I recalled Michael's jibe about Adam having to pack in the dangerous sports. "What was the matter with him?"

There was a long pause. Even Jackson, I noticed, seemed to be waiting intently for the answer. Eventually, Izzy was the one who broke the silence.

"He only told us a month ago that he'd been diagnosed with MND," she said. Her leg had just about stopped bleeding but her face had started to sweat now as the pain and the shock crept in. When I looked blank it was Paul who continued.

"Motor Neurone Disease," he said, sounding authoritative. "It's a progressive degeneration of the motor neurones in the brain and spinal cord. In most cases the mind is unaffected but you gradually lose control of various muscle groups—the arms and legs are usually the first to go. You can never quite tell how far or how fast it will develop because it affects everyone in a different way. Sometimes you lose the ability to speak and swallow. It was such rotten luck! The chances of it happening in someone under forty are so remote, but for it to hit Adam of all people—" he broke off, shook his head and seemed to remember how none of that mattered anymore. "Poor sod."

"It was a tragedy," Izzy said, defiant. "And if I gave him pleasure while he could still take it, what was wrong with that?"

"So," I murmured, "was this a murder, or a mercy killing?"

Diana made a sort of snuffling noise then, bringing one hand up to her face. For a moment I thought she was fighting back tears but then she looked up and I saw that it was laughter. And she'd lost the battle.

"Oh for God's sake, Adam didn't have Motor Neurone Disease!" she cried, jumping to her feet, hysteria bubbling up through the words. "That was all a lie! He *wanted* you to think of him as the tragic hero, struck down at the pinnacle of his youth. And you all fell for it. All of you!"

Paul's face was blank. "So there was nothing wrong with him?" he said faintly. "But he said—"

"Adam was diagnosed HIV-positive six months ago," Diana said flatly. "He had AIDS."

The dismay rippled through the group like the bore of a changing tide. AIDS. The bogeyman of the modern age. I almost saw them edge away from each other, as though afraid of cross-contamination. No wonder Adam had preferred the pretence of a more user-friendly affliction.

And then it dawned on them, one by one.

Izzy realised it first. "Oh my God," she whispered. "He never used…" She broke off, lifting her tear-stained face to Michael. "Oh God," she said again. "I am *so* sorry."

Michael caught on then, reeling away to clutch at the bridge parapet as though his legs suddenly wouldn't support him any longer.

Paul was just standing there, staring at nothing. "Bastard," he muttered, over and over.

Michael rounded on him in a burst of fury. "It's all right for you," he yelled. "You're probably the only one of us who hasn't got it!"

"Ah, that's not quite the case, is it, Paul?" Diana said, her voice like chiselled ice. "Always had a bit of a thing for Adam, didn't you? But he wasn't having any of that. Oh, he kept you dangling for years," she went on, scanning Paul's stunned face without compassion. "Did you really not wonder *at all* why he suddenly changed his mind recently?"

She laughed again. A sound like glass breaking, sharp and bitter. "No, I can see you didn't. You poor fools," she said, taking in all of their devastated faces, her voice mocking. "There you all were debasing yourselves to please him, hoping to bathe in a last little piece of Adam's reflected glory, when all the time he was spitting on your graves."

Michael lunged for her, reaching for her throat. I swept his legs out from under him before he'd taken a stride, then twisted an arm behind his back to hold him down once he was on the floor. *Come on Sam! Where the hell were the police when you needed them?*

I looked up at Diana, who'd stood unconcerned during the abortive attack. "Why on earth did you stay with him?" I asked.

She shrugged. "By the time he confessed, it was too late," she said simply. "There's no doubt—I've had all the tests. Besides, you didn't know Adam. He was one of those people who was a bright star, for all his faults. I wanted to be with him, and you can't be infected twice."

"And what about us?" Paul demanded, sounding close to tears himself. "We were your friends. Why didn't you tell us the truth?"

"Friends!" Diana scoffed. "What kind of friends would screw my boyfriend—or let their girlfriends screw him—behind my back? Answer me that!"

"You never got anything you didn't ask for," Jackson said quietly then, his voice rich with disgust. "The whole lot of you."

Privately, part of me couldn't help but agree with the farmer. "The question is," I said, "which one of you went for revenge?"

And then, across the field, a new-looking Toyota Land Cruiser turned off the road and came bowling across the grass, snaking wildly as it came.

"Oh shit," Paul muttered, "it's Adam's parents. How the hell did they get to hear about it so fast?"

The Land Cruiser didn't stop by the quad bike but came thundering straight onto the bridge itself, heedless of the weight-bearing capabilities of the old structure. It braked jerkily to a halt and the middle-aged couple inside flung open the doors and jumped out.

"Where's Adam?" the man said urgently. He looked as though he'd thrown his clothes on in a great hurry. His shirt was unbuttoned and his hair awry. "Are we in time?"

None of the group spoke. I let go of Michael's wriggling body and got to my feet. "Mr Lane?" I said. "I'm terribly sorry to tell you this, but there seems to have been an accident—"

"*Accident*?" Adam's mother almost shrieked the word as she came forwards. "Accident? What about this?" and she thrust a crumpled sheet of paper into my hands.

Uncertain what else to do, I unfolded the letter just as the first of the police Land Rover Discoveries began its approach, rather more sedately, across the field.

Adam's suicide note was brief and to the point. He couldn't face the prospect of the future, it said. He couldn't face the dreadful responsibility of what he'd knowingly inflicted on his friends. He was sorry. Goodbye.

He did not, I noticed, express the hope that they would forgive him for what he'd done.

I folded the note up again as the lead Discovery reached us and a uniformed sergeant got out, adjusting his cap. Sam was in the passenger seat.

The sergeant advanced, his experienced gaze taking in the shotgun still leaning against the brickwork, Izzy's blood-soaked trousers, and the array of staggered faces.

"I understand there's been a murder committed," he said, businesslike, glancing round. "Where's the victim?"

I waved my hand towards the surviving members of the Dangerous Sports Club. "Take your pick," I said. "And if you want the murderer, well"—I nodded at the parapet where Adam had taken his final dive—"you'll find him down there."

―――――

More to Read!

If you enjoyed this story, then you may also like the earlier Charlie Fox novels, when she is still teaching self-defence in a northern English city. Why not take a look at **CHARLIE FOX: THE EARLY YEARS** eBoxset of books 1, 2, and 3? And please check out the rest of the series **here**.

2

POSTCARDS FROM ANOTHER COUNTRY

THIS WAS the second short story I wrote featuring Charlie Fox.

This story follows my ex-Special Forces turned bodyguard heroine fairly early in her close-protection career, working as part of a security detail for the affluent Dempsey family. Tension is high among Charlie's team after an attempt is made on the life of one of the family, but sometimes the threat comes from an unexpected source, with equally unexpected consequences.

I wrote this story specially to go into the back of the US paperback edition of the fourth Charlie Fox novel, FIRST DROP, as an added extra. This is the only place it has been available previously.

It always bothered me slightly that Postcards From Another Country stood apart from the novel, rather than linking into it in some way. However, when I wrote the ninth book in the series, FIFTH VICTIM, I was finally able to do something about this by using the character of the Dempseys' wayward daughter, Amanda, as one of the integral players in that story. In fact, Charlie's previous history with her made their subsequent relationship far more complex and interesting.

———

SOMEBODY ONCE SAID that the rich are another country—they do things differently there. It didn't take me very long working in close protection to realise that was true. Hell, some of them were a different planet.

The Dempsey family were old money and that put them at the outer reaches of the solar system as far as real-world living was concerned. Personal danger came a distant second to social disgrace, which was always going to make life tough for those of us tasked to keep them from harm.

The family didn't seem bothered so much by the attempted assassination—and that was how they referred to the botched hit that sparked my involvement—so much as the fact it was carried out with no regard to the correct etiquette.

So, they put up with the motion sensors in the grounds and the increased numbers of staff who regularly patrolled the boundaries, but they baulked at having the infrared cameras I'd recommended to blanket the exterior of the house, and absolutely dug their heels in about closed-circuit TV coverage inside. It was my job, I was told firmly, to stop anyone from getting that far. *No pressure, then.*

The radio call came in at just after 3:00 a.m., when I was in the east wing guest suite I'd commandeered as a temporary central control.

"Hey, Charlie, we just apprehended someone in the summer house," came the crackling voice of one of the new guys. "I think you'd better, um, come take a look."

"Stay where you are, Pierce," I said, alerted by the hesitation when he'd been well-briefed on how to handle a situation of this type. "I'm on my way."

The summer house was an architectural flight of fancy writ large. Just goes to show what happens when the wealthy get bored and start doodling.

As I made my way across the lawn and skirted the swimming pool the summer house was lit up like a beacon, lights blazing from every window. I jogged up the steps that led to the ornate entrance and pushed open the door.

As soon as I saw who Pierce had cornered, I understood his reaction. The girl was eighteen but could have passed for twenty-one, and she was utterly beautiful, wearing a mask of blasé bravado and a top that was barely legal. She sat sprawled on one of the cane sofas, one long leg dangling with apparent negligence over the arm. Only the nervous swing of her foot gave lie to her insouciance.

She'd been practising her best sultry pout on Pierce and did not look pleased when I arrived to spoil her fun. Another few minutes and she'd probably have wheedled her way loose. If the scowl she shot in my direction was anything to go by, she realised it, too.

"OK," I said grimly. "I'll deal with this." As he hurried past me, looking flustered, I added quietly, "Stick to procedure, Pierce. And wake the boss."

"Oh…really?" His eyes flicked longingly over the girl before he caught my eye and mumbled, "Yeah, OK, no problem."

As the door closed behind him I turned back and found the girl watching his departure with glittering eyes.

"You've obviously made quite a hit there," I said dryly.

"Hmm," she agreed, letting a secret little smile briefly curve her lips that died when she switched her gaze back to me. "I get the feeling you're not quite so easily impressed, though."

"No, I'm not," I said, and for nearly half a minute we stared each other out. Then I sighed. "It was foolish to think you could get past us, Amanda," I said, voice mild. "Your father hired us because we know what we're doing."

"Damn watchdogs," Amanda Dempsey said with a sneer. "I've been evading people like you, sneaking out, sneaking in, since I was thirteen years old."

"Well, we caught you this time, didn't we?"

"Yes, you did," she drawled and something flashed through the back of her eyes, quick and bright. Then it was gone. She shrugged. "Well, you can't win them all."

She sat up, suddenly restless, and reached for the inlaid ivory antique cigarette box on the glass table in front of her. "Mind if I smoke?"

"Yes," I said, slamming the lid shut before she had a chance to reach inside, and leaving my hand there. Open-mouthed, she thought about making an issue of it, but took one look at my face and decided not to, shrugging like it was of no importance.

"You know that someone tried to kill your father less than a week ago," I went on, allowing some of the exasperation I was feeling to leak through into my voice. "Is this all just a game to you?"

"What if it is?" she said. "Just because someone's decided to take a pot-shot at the old man—and the number of likely suspects must be *legion*—and he's chosen to shut himself off like some old hermit, it doesn't mean *I* have to be a virtual prisoner in this mouldy old place, too, does it?"

The house had every modern convenience. As well as the outdoor swimming pool and the indoor swimming pool, there were tennis courts, stables, a home gym that made the pro place I used seem positively under-equipped, and a dozen full-time staff to pander to the family's every whim. I knew ordinary people who paid a fortune for weekends away somewhere like this. I shook my head. What was that about familiarity and contempt?

"You want to go out, you're free to go by the main gate," I said mildly then. "You don't have to scale the back wall."

"Yeah, right." She gave a cynical snort of laughter and threw me a challenging stare. "So I can go out, huh? Alone?"

I smiled and shook my head. "Not a chance."

"OK, so who'll come out with me and spend the nightclubbing. You?" She let her eyes flick me up and down, deliberately insulting. "What if I get lucky? Are you going to wait outside the bedroom door like a good little watchdog while I—"

"Only if you let me strip-search the guy at gunpoint first," I said easily. "Mind you, some of the guys you've been hanging around with lately are used to that kind of thing, aren't they?"

"How dare you check up on me," she gritted out, her cheeks flushing, a dull red that did nothing for her porcelain skin.

"We checked up on everyone."

She jumped up. For a moment she just stood there, trembling with anger that had her on the verge of tears.

"I should have known you wouldn't take my side," she said, sounding much younger, almost petulant. "My father says 'jump' and the only thing you spineless wimps give a damn about is how high."

"You have to admit that your old man's money has come in very useful for getting you out of a few scrapes over the years," I said cheerfully. "Drug possession and drunk driving, to name but two."

"How much trouble do you reckon I would have got into," she said bitterly, "if I hadn't spent half my life trying to live up to Daddy's impossible ideals?"

"You could have got out from under," I pointed out. "He doesn't exactly keep you locked in the basement."

She laughed, as though I'd suggested something ridiculous. "And done what? Gone where?"

I refrained from rolling my eyes. "You're young and moderately bright. You didn't have to be a lapdog all your life," I said, unable to resist getting my own back for her earlier jibe. "You could have gone anywhere and done anything you set your mind to. Most people," I added, "have to work for what they want in life. They don't get it handed to them on a hall-marked silver platter by a flunky wearing white gloves and a tailcoat."

Amanda paced to one of the windows even though the lights made it impossible to see anything outside except her own reflection in the glass. Maybe that was all she was after. Eventually, she turned back.

"You don't come from money, do you, Charlie?"

I thought of my parents' affluent country home in the stockbroker belt of Cheshire and laughed. "My folks aren't quite down to their last farthing, thank you very much."

I shifted slightly so I was between her and the open doorway, just in case, glancing through it as I did so. Lights had come on in the main wing of the house and I could see figures moving across the lawn. Pierce might be new and green, but it seemed he had remembered what he had to do, at least. "I certainly don't go running to *my* father," I went on, "to bail me out every time I hit a problem."

"If that's what I've done," she said, lip twisting, "it's because I'm just doing what Daddy taught me from the cradle."

"Which is?"

"That money is the answer to everything."

Into the silence that followed, my walkie-talkie crackled into life.

"Hey, Charlie," came Pierce's voice, loud and clear, "you were right. We got him. Some punk kid with a sawn-off. Southwest corner. The situation's contained and the police are on their way."

"Good. Thank you." I put the walkie-talkie back in my pocket and glanced across at the girl. "Sorry, Amanda," I said with no regret in my voice. "Your diversionary tactic didn't work. Who was he, by the way—your latest bit of rough? Did you really think he'd get to your father before we could stop him?"

I put my head on one side and watched her as she turned away from the window and staggered back to the sofa, dropping onto the cushions like her legs would no longer support her. But when she looked up, her eyes were wild, defiant.

"You'll never prove anything," she said. Fine words, spoilt only by the shaky tone.

"She doesn't have to."

Behind me, the door pushed open and her father stepped into the summer house. He wore a silk robe over pyjamas, but he was still a commanding figure.

Amanda stiffened at the sight of him, then dived for the cigarette box on the table in front of her, scrabbling inside it.

"If you're looking for that nice little semiautomatic you hid in there," I said, regretful. "I found it this afternoon."

Her colour fled. She gave a shriek of rage and flew out of her seat. I was never quite sure if it was me or her father she intended to attack, but I didn't give her the chance anyway. Before she'd taken more than two strides I'd grabbed her arms, spun her round, and dumped her back onto the sofa again. I was tempted to get a punch in, but she *was* my principal's daughter, after all.

I settled for a verbal blow instead. "Not so much watchdog, Amanda," I said. "More guard dog."

She snatched up the cigarette box and hurled it instead. It never came close to target, hitting the wall next to the door and cracking in two, scattering filter tips across the Italian tiled floor. Then she began to cry.

Her father regarded this display of temper without expression, while I received another message from Pierce to say the police were at the main gate.

"Let them in," I said. I looked across at Dempsey. "Do you want them to take her, too?"

Dempsey pursed his lips briefly before shaking his head. "That won't be necessary. He motioned with a vague hand. "We'll get her…help of some kind."

"Your decision, sir, of course."

He hadn't taken his eyes off his daughter. "Why, Amanda?" he asked softly. "What do you possibly gain from my death?"

Her lip curled. "My freedom."

He frowned at that. "But you've had everything you could possibly wish for."

"No. I've had everything money could buy," she said in a brittle voice, throwing her head back. "And if you don't know the difference there's no earthly point in my trying to explain it."

There was a long pause. Dempsey finally broke his brooding survey and flicked his eyes at me.

"I'm not dealing with this tonight," he said like it was some minor irritation. "Just get her out of my sight, would you." And with that, he turned on his heel and stumbled from the summer house. It doesn't matter how much money you've got if your children hate you enough to try and kill you. Either for or because of it.

I moved over to his daughter. She rose from the sofa. "Not quite such a game now, is it, Amanda?" I said.

"On the contrary," she said, eyes glittering, head high. "Now it gets interesting."

Like I said: the rich are a whole 'nother country—they do things differently there.

————

More to Read!
If you enjoyed this story, then you may also like the later Charlie Fox novels, where she is in full-blown professional bodyguard

mode. Why not take a look at CHARLIE FOX: BODYGUARD eBoxset of books 4, 5, and 6? And please check out the rest of the series **here**, including FIFTH VICTIM, in which a character from this story makes a return.

3

SERVED COLD

In this collection of short stories featuring Charlie Fox, this story is unusual as it is not written in first person—in Charlie's voice. Instead, the story is that of a waitress and stripper called Layla, who has reached a rock-bottom turning point in her life and has made a momentous decision.

This story came about when Megan Abbott invited me to contribute to the anthology of female noir, A HELL OF A WOMAN, which she was editing. The theme of the anthology was to celebrate the girlfriends, secretaries, sisters and other female characters who normally play side-kicks and walk-ons in noir fiction. This was their chance to shine.

While I was thinking about what to write for A HELL OF A WOMAN, I had a trip planned by ferry from Scotland across to Northern Ireland. It was a long drive to the ferry port at Stranraer, and traffic was slow and heavy. In brief, I just failed to make the boat, arriving at the port as the security gates were closing and I had no choice but to hang around in Stranraer for several hours until the next boat.

This was how I ended up sitting in a little café, drinking a pot of tea and idly watching the waitresses moving mostly ignored between the crowded tables. And that's when the character of Layla first began to form.

She's seen life from the seamy underside, found and lost love, been discarded, betrayed and abandoned. But now she has a plan...

Served Cold was nominated for the Crime Writers' Association Short Story Dagger in 2009, and was chosen to appear in THE MAMMOTH BOOK OF BEST BRITISH CRIME, edited by Maxim Jakubowski.

Also, I revisited one of the characters from this story, who once again becomes Charlie's principal in DIE EASY.

LAYLA'S CURSE, as she saw it, was that she had an utterly fabulous body attached to an instantly forgettable face. It wasn't that she was ugly. Ugliness in itself stuck in the mind. It was simply that, from the neck upwards, she was plain. A bland plainness that encouraged male and female eyes alike to slide on past without pausing. Most failed to recall her easily at a second meeting.

From the neck down, though, that was a different story and had been right from when she'd begun to blossom in eighth grade. Things had started burgeoning over the winter, when nobody noticed the unexpected explosion of curves. But when summer came, with its bathing suits and skinny tops and tight skirts, Layla suddenly became the most whispered-about girl in her class.

A pack of the kind of boys her mother was usually too drunk to warn her about took to following her when she walked home from school. At first, Layla was flattered. But one simmering afternoon, under the banyan and the Spanish moss, she learned a brutal lesson about the kind of attention her new body attracted.

And when her mother's latest boyfriend started looking at her with those same hot lustful eyes, Layla cut and run. One way or another, she'd been running ever since.

At least the work came easy. Depending on how much she covered up, she could get anything from selling lingerie or perfume in a high-class department store to exotic dancing. She soon learned to slip on different personae the same way she slipped on a low-cut top or a demure blouse.

Tonight she was wearing a tailored white dress shirt with frills down the front and a dinky little clip-on bow tie. Classy joint. The last time she'd worn a bow-tie to wait tables, she'd worn no top at all.

The fat guy in charge of the wait staff was called Steve and had hands to match his roving eye. That he'd seen beyond Layla's homely face was mainly because he rarely looked his female employees above the neck. Layla had noted the way his eyes glazed and his mouth went slack and the sweat beaded at his receding hairline, and she wondered if this was another gig she was going to have to try out for on her back.

She didn't, in the end, but only because Steve thought of himself as sophisticated, she realised. The proposition would no doubt come after. Still, Steve only let his pants rule his head so far. Enough to let Layla—and the rest of the girls—know that he'd be taking half their tips tonight. Anyone who tried to hold anything back would be out on her ass.

Layla didn't care about the tips. That wasn't why she was here, anyhow.

Now, she stood meekly with the others while Steve walked the line, checking everybody over.

"Got to look sharp out there tonight, girls," he said. "Mr Dyer, he's a big man around here. Can't afford to let him down."

He seemed to have a thing for the name badges each girl wore pinned above her left breast. Hated it if they were crooked, and liked to straighten them out personally and take his time getting it just so. The girl next to Layla, whose name was Tammy, rolled her eyes while Steve pawed at her. Layla rolled her eyes right back.

Steve paused in front of her, frowning. "Where's your badge, honey? This one here says your name is Cindy and I *know* that ain't right." And he made sure to nudge the offending item with clammy fingers.

Layla shrugged, surprised he picked up on the deliberate swap. Her face might not stick in the mind, but she couldn't take the chance that her name might ring a bell.

"Oh, I guess it musta' gotten lost," she said, all breathless and innocent. "I figured seeing as Cindy called in sick and ain't here —and none of the fancy folk out there is gonna remember my name anyhow—it don't matter."

Steve continued to frown and finger the badge for a moment, then met Layla's brazen stare and realised he'd lingered too long, even for him. With a shifty little sideways glance, he let go and stepped back. "No, it don't matter," he muttered, moving on. Alongside her, Tammy rolled her eyes again.

Layla had the contents of her canapé tray hurriedly explained to her by one of the harassed chefs and then ducked out of the service door, along the short drab corridor, and into the main ballroom.

The glitter and the glamour set her heart racing, as it always did. For a few years, she'd dreamed of moving in these circles without a white cloth over her arm and an open bottle in her hand. And, for a time, she'd almost believed that it might be so.

Not anymore.

Not since Bobby.

She reached the first cluster of dinner jackets and long dresses that probably cost more than she made in a year—just for the fabric, never mind the stitching—and waited to catch their attention. It took a while.

"Sir? Ma'am? Would you care for a canapé? Those darlin' little round ones are smoked salmon and caviar, and the square ones are Kobe beef and ginger."

She smiled, but their eyes were on the food, or they didn't think it was worth it to smile back. Just stuffed their mouths and continued braying to each other like the stuck-up donkeys they were.

Layla had done this kind of gig many times before. She knew the right pace and frequency to circulate, how often to approach the same guests before attentive turned to irritating, how to slip through the crowd without getting jostled. How to keep her mouth shut and her ears open. Steve might hint that she had to put out to get signed on again, but Layla knew she was good and he was lucky to have her.

Well, after tonight, Stevie-boy, you might just change your mind about that.

She smiled and offered the caviar and the beef, reciting the same words over and over like someone kept pulling a string at the back of her neck. She didn't need to think about it, so she thought about Bobby instead.

Bobby had been the bouncer in a roadhouse near Tallahassee. A huge guy with a lot of old scar tissue across his knuckles and around his eyes. Tale was he'd been a boxer, had a shot until he'd taken one punch too many in the ring. Then everything had gone into slow motion for Bobby and never speeded up again.

He wore a permanent scowl like he'd rip your head off and spit down your neck, as soon as look at you, but Layla quickly realised that was merely puzzlement. Bobby was slightly over-matched by the pace of life and couldn't quite work out why. Still plenty fast enough to throw out drunks in a cheap joint, though. And once Bobby had laid his fists on you, you didn't rush to get up again.

One night in the parking lot, Layla was jumped by a couple of guys who'd fallen foul of the 'no touching' rule earlier in the evening and caught the rough side of Bobby's iron-hard hands. They waited, tanking up on cheap whiskey, until closing time. Waited for the lights to go out and the girls to straggle, yawning, from the back door. They grabbed Layla before she had a chance to scream, and were touching all they wanted when Bobby waded in out of nowhere. Layla had never been happier to hear the crack of skulls.

She'd been angry more than shocked and frightened—angry enough to stamp them a few times with those lethal heels once they were on the ground. Angry enough to take their over-flowing billfolds, too. But it didn't last. When Bobby got her back to her rented double-wide, she shook and cried as she clung to him and begged him to help her forget. That night she discov-ered that Bobby was big and slow in other ways, too. And some-times that was a real good thing.

For a while, at least.

"Ma'am? Would you care for a canapé? Smoked salmon and caviar on that side, and this right here's Kobe beef. No, thank *you*, ma'am."

Layla worked the room in a pattern she'd laid out inside her head, weaving through the crowd with the nearest thing a person could get to invisibility. It was a big fancy do, that was for sure. Some charity she'd never heard of and would never benefit from. The crowd was circulating like hot dense air through a fan, edging their way up towards the host and hostess at the far end.

The Dyers were old money and gracious with it, but firmly distant towards the staff. They knew their place and made sure the little people, like Layla, were aware of theirs. Layla didn't mind. She was used to being a nobody.

Mr Dyer was indeed, a big man, as Steve had said. A mover and shaker. He didn't need to mingle, he could just stand there, like royalty, with a glass in one hand and the other around the waist of his tall, elegant wife, looking relaxed and casual.

Well, maybe not so relaxed. Every now and again Layla noticed Dyer throw a little sideways look at their guest of honour and frown, as though he still wasn't quite sure what the guy was doing there.

Guy called Venable. Another big guy. Another mover and shaker. The difference was that Venable had clawed his way up out of the gutter and had never forgotten it. He stood close to the Dyers in his perfectly tailored tux with a kind of secret smile on his face, like he knew they didn't want him there but also knew they couldn't afford to get rid of him. But, just in case anyone thought about trying, he'd surrounded himself with four bodyguards.

Layla eyed them surreptitiously, with some concern. They were huge—bigger than Bobby, even when he'd been still standing—each wearing a bulky suit and one of those little curly wires leading up from their collar to their ear, like they was guarding the president himself. But Venable was no statesman, Layla knew for a fact.

She hadn't expected him to be invited to the Dyers' annual charity ball and had worked hard to get herself on the staff list when she'd found out he was. A lot of planning had gone into this, one way or another.

By contrast, the Dyers had no protection. Well, unless you counted that bossy secretary of Mrs Dyer's. Mrs Dyer was society through and through. The type who wouldn't get out of bed in the morning without a social secretary to remind her. The type whose only job is looking good and saying the right thing and being seen in the right places. There must be some kind of a college for women like that.

Mrs Dyer had made a big show of inspecting the arrangements, though. She'd walked through the kitchen earlier that day, nodding serenely, just so her husband could toast her publicly tonight for her part in overseeing the organisation of the event, and she could look all modest about it and it not quite be a lie.

She'd had the secretary with her then, a slim woman with cool eyes who'd frozen Steve off the first time he'd tried laying a proprietary hand on her shoulder. Layla and the rest of the girls hid their smiles behind bland faces when she'd done that. Even so, Steve took it out on Tammy—had her on her back in the storeroom almost before they were out the door.

The secretary was here tonight, Layla saw. Fussing around her employer, but it was Mr Dyer whose shoulder she stayed close to. Too close, Layla decided, for their relationship to be merely professional. An affair perhaps? She wouldn't put it past any man to lose his sense and his pants when it came to an attractive woman. Still, she didn't think the secretary looked the type. Maybe he liked 'em cool. Maybe she was hoping he'd leave his wife.

At the moment, the secretary's eyes were on their guest. Venable had been free with his hosts' champagne all evening and his appetites were not concerned only with the food. Layla watched the way his body language grew predatory when he was introduced to the gauche teenage daughter of one of the guests, and she stepped in with her tray, ignoring the ominous looming of the bodyguards.

"Sir, can I interest you in a canapé? Smoked salmon and caviar or Kobe beef and ginger?"

Venable's greed got the better of him and he let go of the girl's hand, which he'd been grasping far too long. She snatched it back, red-faced, and fled. The secretary gave Layla a knowing, grateful smile.

Layla moved away quickly afterward, a frown on her face, cursing inwardly and knowing he was watching her. She was here for a purpose. One that was too important to allow stupid mistakes like that to risk bringing her unwanted attention. And after she'd tried so hard to blend in.

To calm herself, to negate those shivers of doubt, she thought of Bobby again. They'd moved in together, found a little apartment. Not much, but the first place Layla had lived in years that didn't need the wheels taken off before you could call it home.

He'd been always gentle with Layla, but then one night he'd hit a guy who was hassling the girls too hard, hurt him real bad, and the management had to let Bobby go. Word got out and he couldn't get another job. Layla had walked out, too, but she went through a dry spell as far as work was concerned, and now there were two of them to feed and care for.

Eventually, she was forced to go lower than she'd had to go before, taking her clothes off to bad music in a cheap dive that didn't even bother to have a guy like Bobby to protect the girls. As long as the customers put their money down before they left, the management didn't care.

Layla soon discovered that some of the girls took to supplementing their income by inviting the occasional guy out into the alley at the back of the club. When the landlord came by twice in the same week threatening to evict her and Bobby, she'd swallowed her pride. By the end of that first night, that wasn't all she'd had to swallow.

Even Bobby, slow though he might be, soon realised what she was doing. How could he not question where the extra money was coming from when he'd been in the business long enough to know how much the girls made in tips—and what they had to do to earn them? At first, when she'd explained it to him, Layla thought he was cool with it. Until the next night when she was out in the alley between sets, her back hard up against the rough stucco wall with some guy from out of town huffing sweat and beer into her unremarkable face.

One minute she was standing with her eyes tight shut, wondering how much longer the guy was going to last, and the next he was yanked away and she heard that dreadful crack of skulls.

Bobby hadn't meant to kill him, she was sure of that. He just didn't know his own strength, was all. Then it was his turn to panic and tremble, but Layla stayed ice cool. They wrapped the body in plastic and put it into the trunk of a borrowed car before driving it down to the Everglades. Bobby carried it out to a pool where the 'gators gathered and left it there for them to hide. Layla even went back a week later, just to check, but there was nothing left to find.

They stripped the guy before they dumped him, and struck lucky. He had a decent watch and a bulging wallet. It was a month before Layla had to put out against the stucco in the alley again.

How were they supposed to know he was connected to Venable? That the watch Bobby had pawned would lead Venable's bone-breakers straight to them?

A month after the killing, Venable's boys picked Bobby and Layla up from the bar and drove them out to some place by the docks. Bobby swore that Layla wasn't in on it, that they should leave her alone, let her go. Swore blind that it was so. And eventually, they blinded him, just to make sure.

Layla thought she'd never get the sound of Bobby's screaming out of her head as they'd tortured him into a confession of sorts. But even when they'd snapped his spine, left him broken and bleeding on that filthy concrete floor, Bobby had not said a word against Layla. And she, to her eternal shame, had been too terrified to confess her part in it all, as though that would make a mockery of everything he'd gone through.

So, they'd left her. She was a waitress, a dancer, a hooker. A no-account nobody. Not worth the effort of a beating. Not worth the cost of a bullet.

Helpless as a baby, damaged beyond repair, Bobby went into some institution just north of Tampa and Layla took the bus up to see him every week for the first couple of months. But, gradually, getting on that bus got harder to do. It broke her heart to do see him like that, to force the cheerful note into her voice.

Eventually, the bus left the terminal one morning and Layla wasn't on it.

She'd cried for days. When she'd gotten word that Bobby had snuck a knife out of the dining hall, waited until it was quiet then slit his wrists under the blankets and bled out softly into his mattress during the night, there had been no more tears left to fall.

Layla's heart hardened to a shell. She'd let Bobby down while he was alive, but she could seek justice for him after he was dead. She heard things. That was one of the beauties of being invisible. People talked while she served them drinks, like she wasn't there. Once Layla had longed to be noticeable, to be accepted. Now she made it her business simply to listen.

Of course, she knew she couldn't go after Venable alone, so Layla had found another bruiser with no qualms about burying the bodies. And, once he'd had a taste of that spectacular body, he was hers.

Thad was younger than Bobby, sharper, neater, and when it came to killing he had the strike and the morals of a rattlesnake. Layla knew he'd do anything for her, right up until the time she tried to move on, and then he was likely to do anything *to* her instead.

Well, after tonight, she wouldn't care.

She slipped out of the ballroom but instead of turning into the kitchen, this time she took the extra few strides to the French windows at the end of the corridor, furtively opened them a crack, then closed them again carefully so they didn't latch.

By the time Layla returned to the ballroom, the canapés were not all she was holding. She'd detoured via the little cloakroom the girls had been given to change and store their bags. What she'd collected from hers she was holding flat in her right hand, hidden by the tray. A Beretta 9mm, hot most likely. As long as it worked, Layla didn't care.

A few moments later someone stopped by her elbow and leaned close to examine the contents of the tray.

"Well hello, *Cindy*." A man's voice, a smile curving the sound of it. "And just what you got there, little lady?"

Thad, looking pretty nifty in the tux she'd made him rent. He bent over her tray while she explained the contents, making a big play over choosing between the caviar or the beef. And underneath, his other hand touched hers, and she slipped the Beretta into it.

"Well, thank you, sugar," he said, taking a canapé with a

flourish and slipping the gun inside his jacket with his other hand, like a magician. When the hand came out again, it was holding a snowy handkerchief, which he used to wipe his fingers and dab his mouth.

Layla had made him practice the move until it seemed so natural. Shame this was a one-time show. He would have made such a partner, someone she might just have been able to live her dreams with. If only he hadn't had that cruel streak. If only he'd touched her heart the way Bobby had.

Poor crippled blinded Bobby. Poor *dead* Bobby...

Ah well. Too late for regrets. Too late for much of anything, now.

Layla caught Thad's eye as she made another round and he nodded, almost imperceptibly. She nodded back, the slightest inclination of her head, and turned away. As she did so she bumped deliberately into the arm of a man who'd been recounting some fishing tale and spread his hands broadly to lie about the size of his catch. He caught Layla's tray and send it flipping upwards. Layla caught it with the fast reflexes that came from years of waiting crowded tables amid careless diners. She managed to stop the contents crashing to the floor, but most of it ended up down the front of her blouse instead.

"Oh, I am *so* sorry, sir," she said immediately, clutching the tray to her chest to prevent further spillage.

"No problem," the man said, annoyed at having his story interrupted and oblivious to the fact it had been entirely his fault. He checked his own clothing. "No harm done."

Layla managed to raise a smile and hurried out. Steve caught her halfway.

"What happened, honey?" he demanded. "Not like you to be so clumsy."

Layla shrugged as best she could, still trying not to shed debris.

"Sorry, boss," she said. "I've got a spare blouse in my bag. I'll go change."

"OK, sweetheart, but make it snappy." He let her move away a few strides, then called after her, "And if that's caviar you're wearing, it'll come out of your pay, y'hear?"

Layla threw him a chastised glance over her shoulder that didn't go deep enough to change her eyes, and hurried back to the little cloakroom.

She scraped the gunge off the front of her chest into the nearest trash, took off the blouse and threw that away, too, then rummaged through her bag for a clean one. This one was calculatedly lower cut and more revealing, but she didn't think Steve would object too hard, even if he caught her wearing it.

She pulled out another skirt, too, even though there was nothing wrong with her old one. This was shorter than the last, showing several inches of long smooth thigh below the hem and, without undue vanity, she knew it would drag male eyes downwards, even as her newly exposed cleavage would drag them up again. With any luck, they'd go cross-eyed trying to look both places at once.

She swapped her false name badge over and took the cheap Makarov 9mm and a roll of duct tape out of her bag. She lifted one remarkable leg up onto the wooden bench and ran the duct tape around the top of her thigh, twice, to hold the nine in position, just out of sight. The pistol grip pointed downwards and she knew from hours in front of the mirror that she could yank the gun loose in a second.

She'd bought both pistols from a crooked military surplus dealer down near Miramar. Thad insisted on coming with her for the Beretta, had made a big thing about checking the gun over like he knew what he was doing, sighting along the barrel with one eye closed.

Layla had gone back later for the Makarov. She didn't have enough money for the two, but she'd been dressed to thrill and she and the dealer had come to an arrangement that hadn't cost Layla anything at all. Only pride, and she'd been way overdrawn on that account for years.

Now, Layla checked in the cracked mirror that the gun didn't show beneath her skirt. Her face was even blander in its pallor and, just for once, she wished she'd been born pretty. Not beautiful, just pretty enough to have been cherished.

The way she'd cherished Bobby. The way he'd cherished her.

She left the locker room and collected a fresh tray from the kitchen. The chefs were under pressure, the activity frantic, but when she walked in on those long dancer's legs there was a moment of silence that was almost reverent.

"You changed your clothes," one of the chefs said, mesmerised.

She smiled at him, saw the fog lift a little as the disappointment of her face cut through the haze of lust created by her body.

"I spilled," she said, collecting a fresh tray. She felt every eye on her as she walked out, smiled when she heard the collective sigh as the door swung closed behind her.

It was a short-lived smile.

Back in the ballroom, it was all she could do not to go marching straight up to Venable, but she knew she had to play it cool. The four bodyguards were too experienced not to spot her sudden surge of guilt and anger. They'd pick her out of the crowd the way a shark cuts out a weakling seal pup. And she couldn't afford that. Not yet.

Instead, she forced herself to think bland thoughts as she circled the room toward him. Saw out of the corner of her eye Thad casually moving up on the other side. The relief flooded her, sending her limbs almost lax with it. For a second, she'd been afraid he wouldn't go through with it. That he'd realise what her real idea was, and back out at the last moment.

For the moment, though, Thad must think it was all going to plan. She stepped up to the Dyers, offered them something from her tray. The secretary still hadn't left his side, she saw. The girl must be desperate.

Layla took another step, sideways toward Venable, ducking around the cordon of bodyguards. Offered him something from her tray. And this time, as he leaned forward, so did she, pressing her arms together to accentuate what nature had so generously given her.

She watched Venable's eyes go glassy, saw the way the eyes of the nearest two bodyguards bulged the same way. There was another just behind her, she knew, and she bent a little further from the waist, knowing she was giving him a prime view of her ass and the back of her newly-exposed thighs. She could almost feel that hot little gaze slavering up the backs of her knees.

Come on, Thad…

He came pushing through the crowd nearest to Venable, moving too fast. If he'd been slower, he might have made it. As it was, he was the only guy for twenty feet in any direction who didn't have his eyes full of Layla's divine body. Venable's eyes snapped round at the last moment, jerky, panicking as he realised the rapidly approaching threat. He flailed, sending Layla's tray crashing to the ground, showering canapés.

The bodyguards were slower off the mark. Thad already had the gun out before two of them grabbed him. Not so much grabbed as piled in on top of him, driving him off his legs and down, using fists and feet to keep him there.

Thad was no easy meat, though. He kept in shape and had come up from the streets, where unfair fights were part of the game. Even on the floor, he lashed out, aiming for knees and shins, hitting more than he was missing. A third bodyguard joined in to keep him down, a leather sap appearing like magic in his hand.

There was that familiar crack of skulls. *Just like Bobby…*

Layla winced, but she couldn't let that distract her now. Her mind strangely cool and calm, Layla stepped in, ignored. The fourth bodyguard had stayed at his post, but Layla was shielded from his view by his own principal, and everyone's attention was on the fight. Carefully, she reached under her skirt and yanked the Makarov free, unaware of the brief burn as the tape ripped from her thigh.

The safety was already off, the hammer back. The army surplus guy down in Miramar had thrown in a little instruction as well. Gave him more of a chance to stand up real close behind her as he demonstrated how to hold the unfamiliar gun, how to aim and fire.

She brought the nine up the way he'd shown her, both hands clasped around the pistol grip, starting to take up the pressure on the trigger, she bent her knees and crouched a little, so the recoil wouldn't send the barrel rising, just in case she had to take a second shot. But, this close, she knew she wouldn't need one, even if she got the chance.

One thing Layla hadn't been prepared for was the noise. The

report was monstrously loud in the high-ceilinged ballroom. And though she thought she'd been prepared, she staggered back and to the side. And the pain. The pain was a gigantic fist around her heart, squeezing until she couldn't breathe.

She looked up, vision starting to shimmer, and saw Venable was still standing, shocked but apparently unharmed. How had she missed? The bodyguard had come out of his lethargy to throw himself on top of his employer, but there was still an open window. There was still time…

Layla tried to lift the gun but her arms were leaden. Something hit her, hard, in the centre of her voluptuous chest, but she didn't see what it was, or who threw it. She frowned, took a step back and her legs folded, and suddenly she was staring up at the chandeliers on the ceiling and she had to hold on to the polished wooden dance floor beneath her hands to stay there. Her vision was starting to blacken at the edges, like burning paper, the sound blurring down.

The last thing she saw was the slim woman she'd taken for a secretary, leaning over her with a wisp of smoke rising from the muzzle of the 9mm she was holding.

Then the bright lights, and the glitter, all faded to black.

————

THE WOMAN LAYLA had mistaken for a secretary placed two fingers against the pulse point in the waitress's throat and felt nothing. She knew better than to touch the body more than she had to now, even to close the dead woman's eyes.

Cindy, the name tag read, under the trickle of the blood. She doubted that would match the woman's driver's licence.

She rose, sliding the SIG semiautomatic back into the concealed-carry rig on her belt. Two of Venable's meaty goons wrestled the woman's accomplice, bellowing, out of the room. She turned to her employer.

"I don't think you were the target, Mr Dyer, but I couldn't take the chance," she said calmly. She jerked her head towards the bodyguards. "If this lot had been halfway capable, I wouldn't have had to get involved. As it was…"

Dyer nodded. He still had his arms wrapped round his wife, who was sobbing, and his eyes were sad and tired.

"Thank you," he said quietly.

The woman shrugged. "It's my job," she said.

"Who the hell are you?" It was Venable himself who spoke, elbowing his way out from the protective shield that his remaining bodyguards had belatedly thrown around him.

"This is Charlie Fox," Dyer answered for her, the faintest smile in his voice. "She's *my* personal protection. A little more subtle than your own choice. She's good, isn't she?"

Venable stared at him blankly, then at the dead woman, lying crumpled on the polished planks. At the unfired gun that had fallen from her hand.

"You saved my life," he murmured, his face pale.

Charlie stared back at him. "Yes," she said, sounding almost regretful. "Whether it was worth saving is quite another point. What had you done to her that she was prepared to kill you for it?"

Venable seemed not to hear. He couldn't take his eyes off Layla's body. Something about her was familiar, but he just couldn't remember her face.

"I don't know—nothing," he said, cleared his throat of its hoarseness and tried again. "She's a nobody. Just a waitress." He took another look, just to be sure. "Just a woman."

"Oh, I don't know," Dyer said, and his eyes were on Charlie Fox. "From where I'm standing she's a hell of a woman, wouldn't you say?"

———

More to Read!

If you liked this, then you may also like the later Charlie Fox novels, where she is in full-blown professional bodyguard mode. Why not take a look at CHARLIE FOX: BODYGUARD eBoxset of books 4, 5, and 6? And please check out the rest of the series **here**, including DIE EASY, in which a character from this story makes a return.

4

OFF DUTY

THIS WAS the fourth short story I wrote featuring Charlie Fox. In this, she and her former boss and now partner, Sean, have moved to New York City and are working for Parker Armstrong's prestigious close-protection agency. But Charlie is on enforced leave—a bodyguard without a body to guard—and feels somewhat adrift.

This story was written specially for the US paperback edition of book six in the series, SECOND SHOT. During the events of that book, Charlie was injured protecting her principal, Simone Kerse, and at the end of it Charlie is still rehabilitating from the double gunshot wounds that almost killed her.

As part of her recuperation, she takes off on her new Buell Firebolt motorcycle and heads for an out-of-season health spa in the Catskill Mountains. There she encounters guests and staff who turn out to be more—or sometimes less—than first meets the eye. Charlie handles them all in her usual inimitable downbeat style.

Incidentally, the damage sustained by the Buell during this story was referenced in the next book in the series—THIRD STRIKE. Only a small mention, but enough for fans to spot!

Instead of appearing as a bonus story at the end of SECOND SHOT, Off Duty was selected for inclusion in CRIMINAL TENDENCIES—GREAT CRIME STORIES FROM GREAT CRIME WRITERS, part of the proceeds of which went to breast cancer charities. The story also appeared in Ellery Queen Mystery Magazine *and was chosen for THE*

Mammoth Book Of Best British Crime 8, edited by Maxim Jakubowski.

———

THE GUY who'd just tried to kill me didn't look like much. From the fleeting glimpse I'd caught of him behind the wheel of his brand new soft-top Cadillac, he was short, with less hair than he'd like on his head and more than anyone could possibly want on his chest and forearms.

That was as much as I could tell before I was throwing myself sideways. The front wheel of the Buell skittered on the loose gravel shoulder of the road, sending a vicious shimmy up through the headstock into my arms. I nearly dropped the damn bike there and then, and that was what pissed me off the most.

The Buell was less than a month old at that point, a Firebolt still with the shiny feel to it, and I'd been hoping it would take longer to acquire its first battle scar. The first cut is always the one you remember.

Although I was wearing full leathers, officially I was still signed off sick from the Kerse job and undergoing the tortures of regular physiotherapy. Adding motorcycle accident injuries, however minor, was not going to sound good to anyone, least of all me.

But the bike didn't tuck under and spit me into the weeds, as I half-expected. Instead, it righted itself, almost stately, and allowed me to slither to a messy stop maybe seventy metres further on. I put my feet down and tipped up my visor, aware of my heart punching behind my ribs, the adrenaline shake in my hands, the burst of anger that follows on closely after having had the shit scared out of you.

I turned, to find the guy in the Cadillac had completed his half-arsed manoeuvre, pulling out of a side road and turning left across my path. He'd slowed, though, twisting round to stare back at me with his neck extended like a meerkat. Even at this distance, I could see the petulant scowl. Hell, perhaps I'd made him drop the cell phone he'd been yabbering into instead of paying attention to his driving...

Just for a second, our eyes met, and I considered making an issue out of it. The guy must have sensed that. He plunked back down in his seat and rammed the car into drive, gunning it away with enough gusto to chirrup the tires on the bone dry surface.

I rolled my shoulders, thought that was the last I'd ever see of him.

I was wrong.

———

SPENDING a few days away in the Catskill Mountains was a spur-of-the-moment decision, taken in a mood of self-pity.

Sean was in LA, heading up a high-profile protection detail for some East Coast actress who'd hit it big and was getting windy about her latest stalker. He'd just come back from the Middle East, tired, but focused, buzzing, loving every minute of it and doing his best not to rub it in.

After he'd left for California, the apartment seemed too quiet without him. Feeling the sudden urge to escape New York and my enforced sabbatical, I'd looked at the maps and headed for the hills, ending up at a small resort and health spa, just north of the prettily-named Sundown in Ulster County. The last time I'd been in Ulster the local accent had been Northern Irish, and it had not ended well.

The hotel was set back in thick trees, the accommodation provided in a series of chalets overlooking a small lake. My physio had recommended the range of massage services they offered, and I'd booked a whole raft of treatments. By the time I brought the bike to a halt, nose-in outside my designated chalet, I was about ready for my daily pummelling.

It was with no more than mild annoyance, therefore, that I recognized the soft-top Cadillac two spaces down. For a moment my hand stilled, then I shrugged, hit the engine kill-switch, and went stiffly inside to change out of my leathers.

———

FIFTEEN MINUTES LATER, fresh from the shower, I was sitting alone in the waiting area of the spa, listening to the self-consciously soothing music. The resort was quiet, not yet in season. Another reason why I'd chosen it.

"Tanya will be with you directly," the woman on the desk told me, gracious in white, depositing a jug of iced water by my elbow before melting away again.

The only other person in the waiting area was a big blond guy who worked maintenance. He was making too much out of replacing a faulty door catch, but unless you have the practice it's hard to loiter unobtrusively. From habit, I watched his hands, his eyes, wondered idly what he was about.

The sound of raised voices from one of the treatment rooms produced a sudden, jarring note. From my current position I could see along the line of doors, watched one burst open and the masseuse, Tanya, come storming out. Her face was scarlet with anger and embarrassment. She whirled.

"You slimy little bastard!"

I wasn't overly surprised to see Cadillac man hurry out after her, shrugging into his robe. I'd been right about the extent of that body hair.

"Aw, come on, honey!" he protested. "I thought it was all, y'know, *part of the service.*"

The blond maintenance man dropped his tools and lunged for the corridor, meaty hands outstretched. The woman behind the reception desk jumped to her feet, rapped out, "Dwayne!" in a thunderous voice that made him falter in conditioned response.

I swung my legs off my lounger but didn't rise. The woman on the desk looked like she could handle it, and she did, sending Dwayne skulking off, placating Tanya, giving Cadillac man an excruciatingly polite dressing down that flayed the skin off him nevertheless. He left a tip that must have doubled the cost of the massage he'd so nearly had.

"Ms Fox?" Tanya said a few moments later, flustered but trying for calm. "I'm real sorry about that. Would you follow me, please?"

"Are you OK, or do you need a minute?" I asked, wary of

letting someone dig in with ill-tempered fingers, however skilled.

"I'm good, thanks." She led me into the dimly lit treatment room, flashed a quick smile over her shoulder as she laid out fresh hot towels.

"Matey-boy tried it on, did he?"

She shook her head, rueful, slicked her hands with warmed oil. "Some guys hear the word *masseuse* but by the time it's gotten down to their brain, it's turned into *hooker*," she said, her back to me while I slipped out of my robe and levered myself, face-down, flat onto the table. Easier than it had been, not as easy as it used to be.

"So, what's Dwayne's story?" I asked, feeling the first long glide of her palms up either side of my spine, the slight reactive tremor when I mentioned his name.

"He and I stepped out for awhile," she said, casual yet prim. "It wasn't working, so we broke it off."

I thought of his pretended busyness, his lingering gaze, his rage.

No, I thought. You *broke it off.*

———

LATER THAT EVENING, unwilling to suit up again to ride into the nearest town, I ate in the hotel restaurant at a table laid for one. Other diners were scarce. Cadillac man was alone on the far side of the dining room, just visible around the edges of the silent grand piano. I could almost see the miasma of his aftershave.

He called the waitress "honey", too, stared blatantly down her cleavage when she brought his food. Anticipating the summer crowds, the management packed the tables in close, so she had to lean across to refill his coffee cup. I heard her surprised, hurt squeak as he took advantage, and waited to see if she'd 'accidentally' tip the contents of the pot into his lap, just to dampen his ardour. To my disappointment, she did not.

He chuckled as she scurried away, caught me watching and mistook my glance for admiration. He raised his cup in my direction with a meaningful little wiggle of his eyebrows. I stared him out for a moment, then looked away.

Just another oxygen thief.

———

As soon as I'd finished eating I took my own coffee through to the bar. The flatscreen TV above the mirrored back wall was tuned to one of the sports channels, showing highlights of the latest AMA Superbikes Championship. The only other occupant was the blond maintenance man, Dwayne, sitting hunched at the far end, pouring himself into his beer.

I took a stool where I had a good view, not just of the screen but the rest of the room as well, and shook my head when the barman asked what he could get me.

"I'll stick to coffee," I said, indicating my cup. The painkillers I was taking made my approach to alcohol still cautious.

In the mirror, I saw Cadillac man saunter in and take up station further along the bar. As he passed, he glanced at my back a couple of times as if sizing me up, with all the finesse of a hard-bitten hill farmer checking out a promising young ewe. I kept my attention firmly on the motorcycle racing.

After a minute or so of waiting for me to look over so he could launch into seductive dialogue, he signalled the barman. I ignored their muttered conversation until a snifter of brandy was put down in front of me with a solemn flourish.

I did look over then, received a smug salute from Cadillac man's own glass. I smiled—at the barman. "I'm sorry," I said to him. "But I'm teetotal at the moment."

"Yes, ma'am," the barman said with a twinkle, and whisked the offending glass away again.

"Hey, that's my kind of girl," Cadillac man called over when the barman relayed the message. Surprise made me glance at him and he took that as an invitation to slide three stools closer, so only one separated us. His hot little piggy eyes fingered their way over my body. "Beautiful *and* cheap to keep, huh?"

"Good coffee's thirty bucks a pound," I said, voice as neutral as I could manage.

His gaze cast about for another subject. "You not bored with this?" he asked, jerking his head at the TV. "I could get him to switch channels."

I allowed a tight smile that didn't reach my eyes. "Neil Hodgson's just lapped Daytona in under one-minute thirty-eight," I said. "How could I be bored?"

Out of the corner of my eye, I saw Dwayne's head lift and turn as the sound of Cadillac man's voice finally penetrated. It was like watching a slow-waking bear.

"So, honey, if I can't buy you a drink," Cadillac man said with his most sophisticated leer, "can I buy you breakfast?"

I flicked my eyes towards the barman in the universal distress signal. By the promptness of his arrival, he'd been expecting my call.

"Is this guy bothering you?" he asked, flexing his muscles.

"Yes," I said cheerfully. "He is."

"Sir, I'm afraid I'm gonna have to ask you to leave."

Cadillac man gaped at us for a moment, then flounced out, muttering what sounded like "frigid bitch" under his breath.

After very little delay, Dwayne staggered to his feet and went determinedly after him.

Without haste, I finished my coffee. The racing reached an ad break. I checked my watch, left a tip, and headed back out into the mild evening air towards my chalet. My left leg ached equally from the day's activity and the evening's rest.

I heard the raised voices before I saw them in the gathering gloom, caught the familiar echoing smack of bone on muscle.

Dwayne had run his quarry to ground in the space between the soft-top Cadillac and my Buell, and was venting his alcohol-fuelled anger in traditional style, with his fists. Judging by the state of him, Cadillac man was only lethal behind the wheel of a car.

On his knees, one eye already closing, he caught sight of me and yelled, "Help, for Chrissake!"

I unlocked the door to my chalet, crossed to the phone by the bed.

"Your maintenance man is beating seven bells out of one of

your guests down here," I said sedately when front desk answered. "You might want to send someone."

Outside again, Cadillac man was going down for the third time, nose streaming blood. I noted with alarm that he'd dropped seriously close to my sparkling new Buell.

I started forwards, just as Dwayne loosed a mighty round-house that glanced off Cadillac man's cheekbone and deflected into the Buell's left-hand mirror. The bike swayed perilously on its stand and I heard the musical note of splintered glass dropping.

"Hey!" I shouted.

Dwayne glanced up and instantly dismissed me as a threat, moved in for the kill.

OK. Now *I'm pissed off.*

Heedless of my bad leg, I reached them in three fast strides and stamped down onto the outside of Dwayne's right knee, hearing the cartilage and the anterior cruciate ligament pop as the joint dislocated. Regardless of how much muscle you're carrying, the knee is always vulnerable.

Dwayne crashed, bellowing, but was too drunk or too stupid to know it was all over. He swung for me. I reached under my jacket and took the SIG 9mm off my hip and pointed it at him, so the muzzle loomed large near the bridge of his nose.

"Don't," I murmured.

And that was how, a few moments later, we were found by Tanya, and the woman from reception, and the barman.

———

"You a cop?" Cadillac man asked, voice thick because of the stuffed nose.

"No," I said. "I work in close protection. I'm a bodyguard."

He absorbed that in puzzled silence. We were back in the bar until the police arrived. Out in the lobby, I could hear Dwayne still shouting at the pain, and Tanya shouting at what she thought of his stupid jealous temper. He was having a thoroughly bad night.

"A bodyguard," Cadillac man mumbled blankly. "So why the fuck did you let him beat the crap out of me back there?"

"Because you deserved it," I said, rubbing my leg and wishing I'd gone for my Vicodin before I'd broken up the fight. "I thought it would be a valuable life lesson—thou shalt not be a total dickhead."

"Jesus, honey! And all the time, you had a gun? I can't believe you just let him—"

I sighed. "What do you do?"

"Do?"

"Yeah. For a living."

He shrugged gingerly, as much as the cracked ribs would let him. "I sell Cadillacs," he said. "The finest motorcar money can buy."

"Spare me," I said. "So, if you saw a guy broken down by the side of the road, you'd just stop and give him a car, would you?"

"Well," Cadillac man said, frowning, "I guess if he was a pal—"

"What if he was a complete stranger who'd behaved like a prat from the moment you set eyes on him?" I queried. He didn't answer. I stood, flipped my jacket to make sure it covered the gun. "I don't expect you to work for free. Don't expect me to, either."

His glance was sickly cynical. "Some bodyguard, huh?"

"Yeah, well," I tossed back, thinking of the Buell with its smashed mirror and wondering who was in for seven years of bad luck. "I'm off duty."

———

More to Read!
If you liked this, then you may also like the later Charlie Fox novels, where she is in full-blown professional bodyguard mode. Why not take a look at CHARLIE FOX: BODYGUARD eBoxset of books 4, 5, and 6? And please check out the rest of the series here, including THIRD STRIKE, book #7, where the damage sustained by her motorcycle in this story gets a mention.

5

TRUTH AND LIES

WHEN I FIRST DECIDED I was going to put together an e-collection (e-thology?) of Charlie Fox stories that became FOX FIVE, I knew I wanted to include something brand new, that had never been seen anywhere else before. As such, this is longer and more detailed than the others—I had no word-counts to restrict me, so I could let Charlie's character have free rein.

I have been deliberately non-specific about the precise location of this tale. It's nowhere and everywhere, both at the same time. There was so much trouble going on, and so many news teams reporting from civil war zones or other areas of conflict that I wanted to write something that was pertinent to them all. I hope I've succeeded.

In this story, Charlie is working as a full-fledged bodyguard for Parker Armstrong's prestigious New York City agency. She is part of a three-man team sent to escort a news reporter, Alison Cranmore, and her cameraman, Nils, out of a beleaguered country on the brink of civil war.

However, things start to go bad very fast and, as the regime begins to disintegrate, it is up to Charlie, with the help of a local fixer, to work out a plan that will get her principals safely across the border.

It comes at a price.

As long as they didn't strip-search me at the airport, I knew I'd be OK. Not that I was trying to bring in anything suspicious, never mind illegal. The government security forces were jumpy enough without giving them more of an excuse to imprison or expel yet another foreigner.

But I *was* attempting to enter the country as a harmless civilian, and I knew if I was forced to undress there was no way anyone could misinterpret my scars. Old knife and bullet wounds are hard to disguise, especially from people who are experts at inflicting them. To me they were a physical reminder of past mistakes—lessons painfully learned and not forgotten.

Three of us had set off from New York twenty-four hours earlier. A rush job—emergency evac. Some news team who'd got in deeper and stayed in longer than was good for them and suddenly needed out. Now. Probably a month after common sense should have told them to leave.

I'd seen it happen before to those exposed to long-term danger. A gradual dulling of the natural flight response until a fifty-fifty chance of living or dying on the job seemed like workable odds.

I had some sympathy with that. Before the evac team left, we'd been briefed by experts on the current political situation here. When they'd told us our chances of survival were not much better, we'd shrugged and carried on packing.

We travelled separately, via half a dozen different neutral countries. I'd dressed with authority rather than intimidation in mind, safely dowdy, and careful to avoid any kind of contact—eye or otherwise—that might have aroused attention. I'd also reverted to my British passport—the one without the Israeli stamps. But in the end, I think the success of my infiltration was down to good old-fashioned chauvinism.

The soldiers who'd taken over the immigration process, with casually slung AKs and obligatory dark glasses, simply did not believe that a woman travelling alone posed any significant threat.

Maybe they were right.

They let me pass with a grubby fondle through my belongings that was cursory at best. Still, as I walked out of the building I was half-expecting the shouted order to stop, to drop to my knees. It was not only the blistering heat of late afternoon which caused the sweat to pool between my shoulder blades.

I ignored the garrulous taxi drivers who pushed and shoved for my notice by the kerb, knew they were weighing up my worth both as a fare and a potential hostage in equal measure. And I kept a firm grip on my bag, even though I was intending to dump it anyway. For now, it was valuable camouflage.

A piercing whistle momentarily silenced the drivers. A man sailed through the crowd towards me, dressed in the local flowing robes. He might once have been handsome, until a large sharp blade—probably a machete—had bisected his face on a ragged diagonal from temple to jaw, destroying the line of his nose and his left eye in the process, and giving him a permanent lop-sided grimace.

The others fell away at the sight of his ruined features. He seemed almost to revel in their revulsion.

"I am Zaki—Zak, yes?" he announced as if I might not recognise him from appearance alone. "We go please, yes?"

"We go," I agreed, and followed him to a dusty Toyota not so much parked as abandoned on the far side of the road. I climbed into the back seat—a pale-haired woman sitting up front beside a local man would have had us pulled over within minutes.

Zak cranked the engine and shot out into traffic without troubling his mirrors. A dented Mercedes, old enough to be a classic, fell into step behind us. The two men in the front seats were wearing dark glasses and identical moustaches. Security forces. Following foreigners was considered something of a national sport.

"Did my…friends arrive yet?" I asked.

Zak shifted in his seat so he could let his good eye roam over me while he drove seemingly more from memory than observation. He shook his head, regretful.

"They did not make it."

All kinds of nasty scenarios flitted through my mind. "Didn't make it *how*, exactly?"

He shrugged, a gesture that involved both hands as well as

shoulders. "They were arrested," he said simply. "It was not to be, yes?"

Shit. So I'm on my own.

"Will they be OK?"

Another shrug. "A few nights in jail. A few bruises, broken bones. Nothing serious. Then they are put on next flight home." The grin broadened. "My government, it does not like mercenaries, yes?"

"We're not mercenaries," I murmured automatically. "We're bodyguards."

Zak's roaming eye lifted to my face for the first time. "You fight and die for money, yes?" he said. "What is difference?"

————

THE HOTEL ROYALE had once boasted an elegant ambience, a blend of western decadence and eastern mystery. It was now a pockmarked survivor with faded paint and barred windows all along the ground floor. The management had placed a number of large concrete blocks outside, making it hard for anyone to take a run at the lobby with a truckful of explosives. A strategy born of experience.

Zak pulled up as close to the entrance as the concrete landscaping would allow. The government watchers in the dented Mercedes hung around long enough to see us get out, then U-turned in the road and headed back for the airport. It was reassuring to know they weren't taking their duties too seriously.

I had a handful of folded dollars ready to pay Zak for the trip —removed discreetly from the money belt around my waist in one of the brief periods when his focus had actually been on the road. He might be my contact here, a man to be trusted—but only to a point. It would not be wise to put undue temptation his way.

As it was, he waited expectantly while I shouldered my bag. I paused a beat, then said, "Could I have my *other* bag, please? I believe you put it in the trunk."

Zak beamed, as if he'd been testing me and could not be more delighted that I'd passed. He opened the Toyota's boot and lifted out a small holdall I'd never seen before. He'd been given careful instructions about what was needed, and I hoped he'd been able to get everything on the list. After all, I could hardly check it right there in the open. Still, it felt reassuringly heavy.

I palmed him the cash and he slammed the boot lid. The sun was almost down and the city would soon be in curfew. A scruffy kid slithered over and tried to con me with a fake bellboy act, gesticulating angrily when I refused to cooperate.

Zak took a step towards him, raising his arms like a bogeyman as his face caught the light. The kid ran. Zak laughed, but there was something hard and bitter behind it.

"I'll see you tomorrow morning—as soon as you can get through," I said. "We're counting on you."

Zak beamed. "Honour is mine, thank you, yes," he said, sketching a small bow.

He jumped into the Toyota and roared away, for all the world like a man who really did think himself honoured, instead of being involved in a crazy suicidal rescue scheme that was already two-thirds down on manpower.

———

IF I'D HAD nerves about the security of the Hotel Royale, they were settled as soon as I entered the lobby area. The occupants of the shabby chic room were three-quarter female and clearly of a professional bent. But if the local hookers felt safe enough to ply their trade here, the chances are it would be OK for the rest of us. For one night, at least.

I signed in under a false name and slipped the manager a hundred when he asked for my passport.

"Thank you, *madame*," he said with a flash of teeth as the note disappeared into his sleeve. "That seems to be in order."

He offered me a room on the ground floor, which I bullied him to change to the third. High enough to make anyone breaking in work for it, but not so high I'd die before jumping if there was a fire. I took the stairs, pausing on each landing to listen for footsteps behind me. There were none.

Safe in my room, I checked the locks and turned on the radio to a raucous local station before finally unzipping the holdall Zak had given me. Inside, as per his instructions, was an assortment of useful items including old clothing, a thin paper map of the city, compass, field medical kit, duct tape, survival knife with a 20cm blade, and an old Sterling Sub-Machine Gun with a spare magazine and two boxes of 9mm rounds. All essentials I dare not risk trying to carry through the airport. Never mind the gun —just having the map and the compass was likely to get me condemned as a spy.

I stripped the Sterling and reassembled it. It had a folding stock that made it short enough to deploy inside a vehicle but gave the shooter some stability for more distant targets. A long time ago I'd trained on just such a weapon, back when the SMG was standard issue to all members of the Women's Royal Army Corps. When I started my Special Forces training we'd moved on to more sophisticated armament, but sometimes simplicity was best.

This old faithful had probably come from India, not in the first flush of youth, but plenty reliable and accurate for the job in hand. Plus, it was sturdy enough to clout someone over the head with if I ran out of ammo. All points in its favour.

I loaded thirty rounds into each magazine rather than topping them off, slotted one into the receiver, and nestled the gun back into the top of the holdall where I could reach it easily if I left the bag partially unzipped. Then I changed into a selection of the shapeless clothes Zak had provided. Somewhat disturbingly, the smell of their last owner still lingered.

Two flights up, the fifth floor had largely been taken over by those hardy or desperate or unbalanced enough among the press contingent to still be in-country. I passed a couple of obvious ex-squaddie contractors who were supposed to be guarding the corridor, but who let me through without a second glance. Black marks all round.

When I banged on the door to the room number as per the briefing, there were signs of rapid movement inside. Shadows came and went behind the Judas glass. Eventually, a man's voice called out curtly, "Who is it?"

I sighed and slid my passport, face down, beneath the door. It was yanked out of my fingers before it was halfway under. For my own safety, I'd brought nothing to identify me as working for Parker Armstrong's New York City close-protection agency. If a Brit ID wasn't enough to convince them, it would just be me and Zak heading for the border tomorrow.

Eventually, the door opened a crack and a narrow section of a woman's face stared out above the chain. She was small and blonde and totally wired. I recognised the slightly freaked-out eyes of someone who is only keeping it together because they don't quite believe what's happening is real.

"Alison Cranmore?" I said, not adding "I presume" because she didn't look like she'd appreciate the Livingstone joke. "I'm Charlie Fox."

The eyes flickered in something that might have been dismay. She closed the door without a word, opening it again a second later, the chain removed. I stepped past her and waited while she fumbled with the chain and lock. I reached into the holdall and picked out another item that had been on Zak's procurement list—a simple wooden doorstop. I slid the narrow end under the door and kicked it into place with the toe of my boot. When it comes to flimsy hotel locks, you can never be too careful.

When I turned, I found Alison had moved back to sit on the bed as if her legs had given out on her, and was staring at me again. She was pretty but not to the point of frivolity, with good bone structure that came across well on camera. Since she'd been in-country, she'd acquired a leaned-down slimness, as if long exposure to heat and stress had stripped her of any excess weight.

The male voice I'd heard belonged to the only other person in the room, a gaunt man sprawled in a chair over by the curtained window. His hair was pale almost to white, and he had the high cheekbones and startling blue eyes that made me think instinctively of Scandinavia.

"*You're* Charlie?" Alison said at last, her voice blankly incredulous.

I looked from her to the man. He was eyeing me with flat amusement, as if his luck had been bad for so long he expected nothing else, and the only recourse left to him was to laugh in the face of it.

"You were expecting some hulking great grunt like that pair outside," I said, jerking my head towards the corridor.

"Too right!" Alison shot back. On the news reports I'd seen her deliver, her voice had a carefully cultivated classlessness, a neutrality designed to convey the information without you noticing the person behind it. Tension made it ragged. "Where are the others? We were told there would be more of you—three or four at least."

I smiled. "Sadly, what you see is what you get."

The blond man spread his hands and shrugged, reminding me of Zak. He'd obviously been in-country a long time. "We are going to die, for sure," he announced, his accent Swedish.

"Not for sure," I said. I reached into the bag and pulled out the SMG, hefted it. "Do you honestly think—if I looked like the gorillas out there—I would have managed to walk in here carrying this?"

———

WE TALKED for a couple of hours. At least, Alison and I talked, while the blond guy—who turned out to be a freelance cameraman called Nils from Stockholm—drank cheap vodka and smoked cigarettes down to the knuckle.

At the end of it, I knew more than I wanted about the injustices going on inside the country, and less than I needed about the situation we were in. I was already aware that the president was a poster-boy for corrupt dictators the world over. The current unrest was being generated by his former right-hand man, who had somehow managed to survive being purged to mount the first viable opposition in years. Beyond that, I didn't need to know the details.

"So," I said. "What's stopping you going out the same way I came in—via the airport on the first commercial flight to just about anywhere?"

Nils harrumphed into his shot glass—no easy feat. "This is what they are waiting for," he said.

I glanced at Alison. "You think the government would try to prevent you leaving?"

It was Nils who answered. "No way," he said. "It is their dream that we go—get us out of their head."

I was pretty sure he meant 'hair', but I didn't correct him. Mainly because his English was a hell of a lot better than my grasp of Swedish, which was limited to mild obscenities and ordering beer.

"So," I repeated, "what's stopping you?"

"They'll let *us* go, but not the story," Alison said.

"You've been here for six months, sending out stories all the time," I said. "What's special about this one?"

That's when they began to act cagey. And shortly thereafter, I began to lose my patience.

Eventually, I returned to my room on the third floor, having told Alison and Nils to be ready to move as soon as curfew lifted in the morning. As I left, I suggested quietly to Alison that she try and separate Nils from his bottle of vodka before he hit the bottom—mentally and physically. Some people get maudlin when they drink. Clearly, Nils was one of them.

I tried not to let the cloak and dagger attitude irritate me. It's not unusual for clients to try to keep you in the dark. I suppose they made the same assumption as Zak—that they've bought your services and so can anyone else, if the price is right.

The reality is that the close-protection business is all about reputation, and Parker Armstrong's outfit had a name for utter reliability. With the rest of my team blown, the responsibility for maintaining that reputation rested squarely on my shoulders.

No pressure, then.

————

I woke in the middle of the night to find I'd rolled out of bed on a reflex and grabbed for the SMG which I'd left close to hand on the side table. I lay there on the floor, hard up against the side of the mattress with my heart hammering against my breastbone and my ears straining in the dark.

For a moment I wondered if I'd merely been in the grip of

some weirdly realistic nightmare. Then the noise that had woken me came again. Incoming fire—close proximity.

Keeping low, I crabbed over to the window, slithered up the wall alongside it and peered out. Tracer rounds were arcing through the night from the south, aimed not for the city itself, but further east. I didn't need GPS to work out they were targeting the airport.

Ah well, there goes that *escape plan.*

There had been plenty of collateral damage before the gunners got their eye in. Isolated fires were dotted all over the city, their flames licking up into the night sky until the underside of the clouds themselves seemed to be burning.

Through the single-glazed window I could hear the distinctive rattle of AK fire in the streets below. It was this development, I knew, that had penetrated my subconscious. The AK was the weapon of choice for all sides in this conflict, so it was hard to know who was shooting at what.

I considered our options. The hotel itself did not seem to be a direct target. Moving in the dark would be ludicrous. Staying put was the only logical choice.

I wrapped myself in several layers of spare clothing and crawled to the far side of the bed, away from the window and possible shrapnel, with the holdall close to hand and the SMG cradled in my arms. If the worst happened and the building collapsed around me, the bed would not be squashed completely flat, creating a survival pocket alongside it. And if we received a direct hit, well, there wasn't much I could do.

Either way, I didn't intend to lose sleep over it.

———

ON THE GROUNDS that you should never pass up the opportunity to eat, I was down in the lobby early the following morning in hopes of breakfast, only to find Alison and Nils had beaten me to it.

Alison gave me a wan smile as I sat down at their table.

"I never could sleep through a bombardment," she said. And

as if to highlight her point of view, another distant explosion rumbled in.

Nils looked the worse for wear, too, but that could simply have been down to fallout from the night before's vodka.

"You might want to change before we leave," I told him. He was wearing digital-desert pattern trousers and a khaki shirt.

"What for?"

I shrugged. Zak must be rubbing off on me, too. "You look like a soldier," I said. "We're going to have enough trouble getting out of here without both sides mistaking you for an enemy combatant."

Nils grunted. He took a sip of coffee the colour and consistency of road tar, and said with a certain arrogance, "This is why we have you."

"Actually," I said mildly, "this is why *she* has me. You're just along for the ride."

Alison blinked. "But—?"

"It was *your* news agency who contracted us—Nils is freelance," I told her, flicked my eyes across both of them and added with as much diplomacy as I could manage, "I'll do my best to keep everyone safe, but if it comes down to it, I am bound to protect Alison first."

"And I get to go fuck myself into a cocked hat," Nils said morosely.

The intricacies of that manoeuvre were lost on me, but I got the gist. "That is your prerogative," I agreed. "But it doesn't mean I'm going to let you do the same to the rest of us." I let that settle, then put effort and quiet force into my voice. "Now—go and change."

The Swede sat for a moment, anger swirling behind his features, then he got up without a word and strode away towards the lobby. AK fire in a neighbouring street seemed to echo in time with his footsteps.

I'd noticed that the lobby area had been crowding up—it seemed we were not the only ones proposing to make a rapid exit in light of the collapsing situation. The manager didn't look unduly upset by the exodus. I gathered that there would soon be a new influx of war zone junkies to replace those leaving. Not just news teams, but private military contractors, too. Some of them were legit, but some of them were just gun freaks who wanted a chance to take out a live moving target without spending the rest of their life behind bars for the privilege.

Probably best to be gone before any of them arrived.

Alison leaned across and touched my arm. "I *need* Nils," she said, low and urgent. When I raised an eyebrow, she flushed. "Not like that. I need him for this story. Without him, I have nothing. It's just *my* word, you know?"

I stared at her. "You mean you don't have proof?"

"Oh, we have proof," she said. "On digital video—*Nils's* video. And without it, they'll say I've gone completely off my rocker."

"Couldn't you have beamed it out by satellite or something, if it's so important?"

"Nils won't let go of it. He says that once it's out there, anybody could steal it."

"Better that than never getting the damn thing out at all."

She gave an unhappy shrug, the reporter in her understanding Nils's reluctance to let go of his baby for anyone to exploit.

I would have pushed her for more, but the Swede's return made her clam up completely. His manner was one of sulky confidence, as if he knew exactly what Alison might have told me during his absence. Still, at least he *had* changed, into a flowered shirt and blue lightweight hiking trousers with the lower half of the legs zipped off to turn them into comically long shorts. He'd gone from looking like a weekend warrior to a bad tourist.

"So, when do we go?" he demanded.

That was a question I'd been hoping nobody was going to ask. Zak was late. Not just 'delayed'—even by the generally relaxed timekeeping standards of this place—but seriously, worryingly, late. Time edged round. Other breakfasters came and went. I began to think I might have to resort to Plan B, which was basically to steal an abandoned vehicle and make a run for it by ourselves.

About half an hour later, I spotted the two moustachioed

watchers from the dented Merc, who slid into the lobby and were loitering conspicuously behind the drooping fronds of a potted palm. I swear hotels only include potted palms in their decor for exactly this purpose. I silently christened them Twee-dle-Dumb and Tweedle-Dumber.

I tried not to read too much into their arrival. Maybe they figured it was safer here than out on the streets when they were so clearly aligned with the current regime. And maybe Zak's alarm clock had failed to go off and he'd simply overslept.

Yeah, right.

————

JUST WHEN I'D begun to seriously consider luring the Tweedle brothers outside and nicking their Merc, Zak finally turned up, looking freshly showered. He was full of shrugs and bows and apologies as he led us out to his old Toyota, which also now glistened wetly in the morning heat.

"*Please* tell me you didn't stop to wash your car," I said.

He gave another of his voluminous shrugs. "Water cannon, yes?"

I gathered from the huge cracks in the windscreen and the sopping interior that he wasn't joking. The front seats had taken the brunt. This made Nils even more grumpy when I pointed out that, strictly for propriety's sake, Alison and I should ride in the back.

We loaded our gear. I'd transferred anything I needed from my original luggage to the holdall Zak had provided, and abandoned my old bag in my room for the cleaning staff to make use of or sell, as they wished. I'd left the bag carefully spread open on my bed—people were having a bad enough time here without adding an unnecessary bomb scare into the mix.

As we climbed into the Toyota, the Tweedles emerged and trotted towards their own car with much surreptitious glancing in our direction. People had been leaving since curfew lifted and the pair hadn't taken much notice, which meant they had been specifically waiting for us.

Not good.

I leaned forwards and tapped Zak on the shoulder. "Do you have any friends you can rely on who might help us?" I asked.

He pursed his lips, torn between being paid for his own help-fulness and being forced to split whatever money I was prepared to spend. "Maybe yes, maybe," he said at last.

"Call them," I said. "Tell them to steal or borrow a car and be ready to move." With reluctance, Zak dragged out an ancient mobile phone the size of a brick, and prodded in a number. As he waited for the connection, I tapped his shoulder again. "Oh, the car—make sure they take it from someone they don't like."

———

I DON'T KNOW if the antiquity of Zak's phone had anything to do with it, but he was unable to get through to his friends. "Net-work is down," he announced casually over his shoulder as we careered out into traffic. "We need to make side-show to go see them, yes?"

I glanced out of the rear screen. Beads of water still rolled down the outside of the glass, and every time Zak cornered both front seats squelched. The Merc had slotted in behind us as if on a long tow. The Tweedle brother in the passenger seat was talking on his own phone, arms waving wildly as he did so. Put handcuffs on half the guys in this part of the world and they'd be struck instantly mute.

"Our watchers are back and they appear to be spreading the word." I stabbed a thumb over my shoulder towards our tail. "I thought you said the network was down."

Zak looked pained. "*Civilian* network is down," he explained, twisting in his seat without regard for obstacles in the road like burning buses and strewn rubble from the occasional half-collapsed building.

Alison spun back from staring out of the rear window. We'd both covered our face and hair with local scarves, so all I could see of her was a pair of accusing eyes. "You *knew* you were being followed?" she demanded.

"Everyone is followed *to* the hotel," I said. "Looks like they really don't want to see you leave." I unzipped the holdall, which sat alongside me on the rear seat, and brought out the SMG, keeping it below the level of the glass. "Do you know how to load a magazine?"

She shook her head.

"Don't worry," I said grimly, "you'll soon learn."

———

THE CITY WAS a mix of wide, open squares and narrow twisting streets. It was as if the head of planning had grand designs, but the rest of the committee conspired against him during his lunch hour, surreptitiously crowding houses and offices and shops into every available space.

Zak tore through the open areas as if trying to avoid a missile lock. Some of the squares were still awash, but at least it was only water.

Water cannon…

"Why didn't they just shoot you?" I asked suddenly.

"Thank you, please, yes?" Zak queried over his shoulder. I'd noticed that if he didn't understand the question, he tended to just throw words at you, hoping to land on the right answer by a process of elimination.

"There's been artillery fire all over the city during the night. If it was government forces—and I can't see the rebels bothering with water cannon—why didn't they just shoot at you?"

"Too many news peoples," Zak said, his grin becoming wider and slightly more grotesque. "Both sides wanting support of international community, yes?"

"Water cannon looks bad enough on camera," Nils said from the front seat, where he was bracing himself during the wild ride with both hands and a knee wedged hard against the dashboard. "But killing civilians looks worse, for sure." And the bitterness was back in his voice again.

Zak swerved round a corner and a shabby café came into view, one window boarded up with corrugated iron sheeting and bullet pockmarks in the walls. Outside was a motley collection of cars and scooters. They weren't so much parked as huddled together like flotsam in the corner of a dirty harbour.

"Ah, luck is with us," cried Zak, taking both hands off the wheel in his delight. "My friend—he is here."

He ran the Toyota into the melee until the bumper docked with the car in front, and jumped out before I could stop him. I cursed under my breath. Going after him meant leaving the gun behind—carrying it openly would be inviting trouble. I went after him with a wad of money folded tight in my hand, leaving the SMG on the back seat for now and my door open. I had already tucked the survival knife through my belt, hidden beneath the folds of baggy clothing, and I made sure my scarf was pulled tight around my face.

The dented Merc pulled up on the other side of the street. This area was not a government stronghold, and the Tweedles looked as out of place here as they did uneasy.

They were so close I had to keep my voice low as I explained to Zak what was needed. If the Tweedles had wound down their windows, they could have joined in without needing to shout. These guys must have called in sick the day the Beginners' Guide to Discreet Surveillance class was run.

Zak disappeared the cash with a magician's skill and hurried into the café, sandals flapping. I gave the street a slow once-over, then climbed back into the Toyota, still leaving my door open.

"Where's he gone?" Alison demanded.

"We need some help to get rid of our tail before we run for the border," I said, eyes sliding towards the Tweedles. "As it is, if those two follow any closer we'll be able to slap them with a paternity suit."

Nils frowned, nodded to the gun by my leg. "So—why not shoot them?"

There was any number of tactical reasons why that would be a Very Bad Plan but before I could explain any of them, Alison rounded on him. "Is that how we get our story out now—kill whoever gets in our way?" she asked. "We're supposed to report the problems, not become a part of them, remember?"

Nils gave another shrug that would have done Zak proud, and slumped back into his seat. The sudden silence between us grated. Alison muttered, "Come *on*, come on," under her breath. "What's taking him so long?"

I reckoned she'd been here long enough to realise that every business transaction started with drawn-out cups of tea or evil coffee. But even I didn't like the time Zak had been inside. If nothing else, the distant AK fire that had formed a constant backdrop seemed to be growing in pitch and volume. And the deserted street was not quite so deserted anymore. There were faces, movement, in once-deserted doorways and windows around us. I kept a wary eye on the slow convergence.

The Tweedle brothers were becoming increasingly agitated, too, to the point where I entertained a vain hope they might jump ship without waiting for further discouragement. They clearly weren't happy with their current location, though—a fact which was not lost on Alison.

She ducked in her seat to get a better look at the buildings surrounding us, as if getting her bearings for the first time since the journey had begun. "This Zak—whose side is he on?" she asked abruptly.

"His own, I think," I said. "If you think he might sell us out, I agree that's crossed my mind, but this is a strictly cash-on-delivery kind of job. His promised fee is waiting for him at the border, so it's in his best interests to get us there."

Not to mention what I'll *do to him if he tries anything…*

She nodded, and then I had to open my big mouth to add, "If it helps, I don't think he's a closet admirer of *El Presidente*."

She didn't flinch. Flinching would imply involuntary movement. Instead, she went utterly still, like a fat rabbit who's suddenly realised that hawk-shaped shadow directly overhead is not a novelty cloud formation.

"We need to get out of here," she said, a fine serration of panic sawing through her voice. "It's not safe—"

"Get a grip," I snapped, surprised and not a little annoyed by the cracks in her cool. "Of course it's not *safe*. We're in a country that's had months of unrest and is heading downhill rapidly into full-blown civil war. Not exactly Leamington Spa on a wet Bank Holiday Monday."

"You don't understand," she said. She broke her immobility, twisting as if trying to cover all angles at once. "We can't trust him! We need to go."

I confess I'd been reluctantly edging towards a similar conclusion, but maybe with slightly less hysteria. I ducked my head to check the Toyota's ignition. It was empty.

Shit.

"OK," I said, "Let's—"

Before I got any further, a trio of skinny figures slithered out of a narrow alley next to the café and approached the car from the driver's side, peering in. They were mid-teens, but I didn't make the mistake of thinking of them as children. Nevertheless, although I put my hand on the SMG I kept it hidden—for now.

"English? American?" they demanded. "Manchester United? Red Sox?"

"No, Swedish," Nils called back. And then, perhaps realising that replying in English might not have been too smart, added quickly, "*Jag är Svensk. Svensk!*"

"*Français,*" Alison declared, not to be outdone.

The pair ducked to look directly at me. "Irish," I said, putting all the threat of East Belfast into the single word.

They paused, not quite sure what to make of our replies. I flicked my gaze briefly to the café, the open doorway now thronged with faces watching the show. Nothing like the possibility of a lynching to brighten a dull morning.

I felt my heart rate step up, adrenaline pumping. I knew that when things went bad here, they tended to reach flashpoint very quickly. Zak might be setting us up, or he might be lying inside the building with his throat cut. Alternatively, he could be sipping his mud coffee and navigating the formal dance of small talk on his way to a deal.

Hope for the best, but plan for the worst.

I glanced around me, forcing my focus outwards to assess the whole scene. The Merc was only metres away with the engine running. It was a heavy vehicle—heavy enough to use as a battering ram if I needed to force our way through. If it came to it, I would have to take out the Tweedles and to hell with Alison's sensibilities. Still, the prospect of getting my principals transferred from one vehicle to the other, in the face of hostile and no doubt readily armed opposition, was not a choice to be made lightly.

"Maybe we should ask those watching us to watch *over* us?" Nils suggested out of the corner of his mouth. He'd twisted in his seat and followed my gaze—if not my intent—to the pair in the Merc.

"Not exactly what I had in mind," I murmured. "Just be ready to move."

Then, just as I tightened my fingers around the pistol grip of the Sterling, Zak pushed his way through, talking loudly, waving his arms as if to shoo away crows. The youths scattered and Zak climbed back into the car.

"All OK," he said, smiling. "We go, yes?"

He rammed the gear lever in reverse and the Toyota leapt back from the pile of vehicles, coming within a gnat's whisker of whacking another dent into the side of the Mercedes as it did so.

Tweedle-Dumb, behind the wheel, rapidly shifted the big car backwards away from a collision. Maybe any damage was deducted out of his pay. Looking at the state of the Merc, he hadn't received his full packet in quite a while.

Meanwhile, a nondescript car turned into the street behind us and approached so fast I thought the driver was going for full ramming speed. I was just about to call a warning when Zak shoved the Toyota's transmission into first and stamped on the accelerator. We shot off with the second car so close up behind us I couldn't see enough of the front grille to identify the make. The Merc wheelspun in pursuit.

The Tweedles could not have been happy about having this buffer between us. The two rear cars weaved from side to side in the narrow street in an attempt to pass or avoid being passed. All it needed was sets of running boards and men in pinstripe suits and I'd be in the middle of a classic Chicago gangster movie.

Looking out of the back window, all I could see of the chase car's occupants was their eyes. There were four people inside—that they were all men was a fairly safe bet—with their faces covered. If their gesticulating arms were anything to go by, they were all talking at once. Even the driver.

"Hold very tight please, thank you, yes," Zak yelled over his shoulder, then spun the wheel to launch us into an alleyway with barely half a metre spare on either side. The chase car followed, slicing off its door mirrors as it ricocheted through the entrance.

The alley was lined with houses, narrow doorways that spilled straight out into the roadway. I prayed nobody stepped out of their front door as we thundered past.

I turned to look back, just in time to see the nose of the chase car dip as the driver slammed on the brakes. The front wheels locked, smoke and dust billowing up, until the car finally came to a halt. All four doors opened. All four occupants leapt out. They scarpered into the nearest buildings, which swallowed them up as if they'd never been, leaving a stalled roadblock firmly in the path of the Mercedes.

We burst out of the far end of the alley and fishtailed away, leaving the Merc boxed in behind us.

Zak turned and grinned at me hugely over his shoulder. "My friends, they follow plan, yes?" he said.

"Absolutely," I agreed.

Nils had twisted to watch the foiled pursuit. For the first time, I thought I caught a glimpse of bone-dry humour. "*You* planned this?"

I shrugged. "Only works if you've got a chase car following close behind," I said. "But if Princess Di's security had done the same instead of trying to outrun the paparazzi that night in Paris, who knows how things might have turned out?"

Zak kept his foot wedged down on the throttle and made a series of random turns. With every passing minute, the Tweedles' chances of reacquiring us diminished until they were somewhere between slim and none.

I wondered if they'd have that taken out of their pay, too.

———

WE DROVE for nearly three hours through the hottest part of the day. The Toyota's air conditioning system consisted of opening the windows. At speed, the inrush of dust and grit blowing across the raised desert highway acted like the roughest facial you ever had. After the first ten minutes, my eyes were full of gravel, but it was preferable to dying of heat exhaustion.

Alison had calmed down after her panic outside the café. In a manner that always struck me as terribly English, she attempted to over-compensate for doubting Zak's allegiances earlier by being extra nice to him now, giving his every pronouncement more attention than it warranted, smiling and nodding.

Zak, as if to demonstrate his debonair side, had the radio tuned to a local station and was singing along. By that, I mean he was singing at the same time *as* the music, rather than in time *with* it. His accompanying hand slaps on the steering wheel were equally erratic.

Nils coped with the racket by feigning sleep. I could tell by the way his chest rose and fell that he was faking it.

The road was heavy with traffic, foot as well as vehicle. There were the ubiquitous boys on donkeys, overladen pickup trucks with vociferous goats in the back, mixed in with new BMWs and SUVs. Hardly anyone was heading towards the city. The flood of refugees had started—all making for the border just like us.

"We need to get off highway, yes?" Zak suggested over the roar of wind noise as we slowed for yet another broken-down donkey.

I hadn't missed the fact that when we *weren't* moving, we were attracting the wrong kind of attention from our fellow travellers. Their country's conflict might be mainly internal, but that didn't mean they'd pass up the chance to stone a group of foreigners, just for someone else to blame.

"You wouldn't by any chance know an alternative route, would you?"

Zak turned to look at me, his distorted features pulled almost into a leer. "Maybe yes, maybe," he said.

———

ZAK'S alternative route involved the kind of terrain I'd only previously encountered on army tank courses. It was brutal, but the old Toyota scrambled gamely on, encouraged by Zak's random wheel-slapping and tuneless yodels. Nils feigned coma by this time. I was tempted to join him.

Eventually, just when I thought my eyes would never line up

with their sockets ever again, we bumped off the rutted track and re-joined something that nearly resembled a metalled road.

"All OK now, yes?" Zak said, beaming at us as he put his foot down.

It was clear that he was not the only one who knew about this detour, but at least the traffic was light and the slow-moving stuff kept to the shoulder to let us by. We were moving through sparse desert scrub, flanked by huge outcrops of rock blasted smooth by the elements. Settlements huddled close to the road-side as if fearful of what lay beyond it, out in the wilderness. The few people we saw stared at the passing vehicles like floats in a parade. They were mainly women, kids, and the elderly—over here that seemed to encompass anyone over the age of thirty-five.

Where are the men?

"How far to the border?" Alison asked.

"Not far," Zak said with a vague gesture to the road ahead that could have indicated anything from an hour to a week. "All OK now."

The road had begun to twist around the rock formations, creating natural chokepoints and elevated strongholds that made my defensive antennae twitch like crazy. And maybe it was because this was one of the rare occasions when Zak actually had his eye on his driving so I couldn't see his face, but something in his voice worried me. A tightness, a faint harmonic that had been absent during the rest of our journey.

He's nervous, I realised. *Why now?*

I sat forwards in my seat. "Any likely problems up ahead I should know about?"

"No, no, all OK, thank you, yes."

There it was again—more of it this time.

Fear.

"Zak, stop the car."

"No, we must go," he insisted, sweat in his voice now. "All OK."

"What is it?" Alison demanded. "What's wrong?"

That's what I'm trying to find out.

Desperate measures were called for.

"Stop the car or I'll pee here," I improvised loudly. "Your choice, but it's going to stink."

Zak flung me a single horrified glance over his shoulder and stood on the brakes.

We were in the middle of a corner at the time and the Toyota didn't take kindly to the manoeuvre, skating on the loose gravel that coated the road until we eventually came to an untidy halt.

Still, in other ways the timing couldn't have been better. Up front, about three hundred metres in the distance, was a narrow bridge across a dried-up riverbed. The entrance to the bridge was currently blocked by a line of rusted oil drums. A dusty Land Cruiser with vaguely military markings sat nearby. Guarding the drums was a group of four guys in sloppy fatigues. The only thing impressive about these troops was their obvious familiarity with the weapons they carried.

"You didn't mention we'd have to pass through any checkpoints on this road," I said.

Zak gave a subdued shrug. "They come and they go," he said, striving for the philosophical air of someone describing the seasons. "All the time."

I moved my face closer to his ear, shifting the SMG across and into my hands at the same time. "Are you sure about that?"

"Of course he is sure," Nils said impatiently, reaching for his passport and papers from the outside pocket of his rucksack. "We stop, we give them money, and they let us pass. Like the man said—it happens all the time."

"On a side road in the middle of nowhere?" I said, not taking my eyes off Zak. "With no backup nearby?"

Zak didn't answer but I saw his Adam's apple dip rapidly in his skinny throat. Meanwhile, one of the slower vehicles we'd passed—a battered pickup, its exhaust smoking like a wet bonfire—overhauled us and lumbered towards the roadblock. The soldiers tensed for a moment, clutching their weapons, then rolled the drums aside and waved the pickup on.

"Well, they do seem to be letting people through," Alison said.

"Either that," I said, "or they're waiting for someone in particular."

She frowned. "We can't go back, so...what do we do now?"

My turn to shrug. However tempting it was to push on regardless, sometimes going back was by far the most sensible—and safest—option. But, still...

"We go forwards," I said.

Zak stretched an arm to put the Toyota into gear. As he did so, I slid the SMG across my lap and jammed the muzzle hard into the back of Zak's seat. The elderly Toyota had only a passing nod to lumbar support, and I knew from the way he arched that Zak had not only felt it, he knew exactly what it was. He tensed in automated response, and then relaxed.

"Is all OK, no problems," he said and before I could react he'd stuck his head out of his open window, yelling, "Unarmed! We are unarmed." And he launched into more of the same in several different local dialects.

What the hell...?

I gave him a vicious prod with the gun through the thin seat back. "Zak, shut up."

"Is OK," he said again, a patent untruth as the soldiers readied their weapons in front of us.

What happened next is known as the tachy-psyche effect. The way time slows in moments of duress as if squashed and stretched by the extreme pressure.

Tick.

Suddenly, between one second and the next, I had all the time in the world to assess the situation. Apparently random images flashed through my consciousness in a continuous stream that flowed to form a single bright cohesive strand.

All the soldiers at the checkpoint were wearing army uniforms that didn't quite fit, as if borrowed from another owner —with or without consent. Their vehicle could have been a mock-up or simply stolen. They should have been carrying standard-issue AKs, but only two were armed with the classic assault rifle. One of the others had what looked like an old Mac-10, and the fourth cradled a 9mm SMG.

Just like the one in my hands—the one Zak had supplied. The one he seemed so relaxed about when I jammed it against his spine...

Tick.

Although I'd put thousands of rounds through similar weapons in my time, I'd had no chance to test-fire this particular SMG, and there are plenty of ways to subtly sabotage a gun that would not be immediately obvious—even during the strip-down inspection I'd given it the night before.

A few fractions of a mil shaved off the firing pin and all I'd get when I squeezed the trigger would be the dull clack of the mechanism trying to strike the primer cap of the first round, which would be just out of reach. No primer cap detonation, no ignition of the main charge, no projectile leaving the end of the barrel.

It was a good job the SMG *was* sturdy enough to use as an emergency club, because if my suspicions were correct, that was all it was good for.

Tick.

I let go of the gun and ripped the survival knife out of concealment, firm in the knowledge that there's not much you can do to interfere with a knife that isn't obvious, especially if you've spent time checking the blade is sharp.

This blade was plenty sharp enough to pierce the thin vinyl back of the Toyota's seat, slice through the flimsy internal padding, and out again through the front. I only stopped when I felt the point's resistance as it entered skin and flesh.

This time, Zak jerked forwards with a hoarse cry. I snaked my left arm around the headrest and clamped my forearm hard across his throat, gripping the other side of the headrest to keep him pinned there.

Alison, sitting alongside me, had an unobstructed view. "Charlie!" she shouted, aghast. "What the hell are you *doing?*"

"Shut up," I said calmly. "Zak—drive."

———

ZAK DID NOTHING. He simply sat, with the tip of the knife he'd given me now embedded in his back.

"I cannot," he said at last. "I am very sorry." The clown personae he adopted to fit his bizarre distorted appearance dropped away. His voice was different again, less ingratiating, more dignified. He sounded resigned, too, as if the fates had taken things out of his hands and he was OK with that.

Two of the soldiers started to approach us, yelling for us to not move, to get out of the car, to put our hands up, to lie on the floor. I resisted the urge to shout, "Make up your minds!"

I slid the knife out of Zak and his seat, shifted my grip and laid the blade across his right cheek, close to his one remaining eye. His eyelid twitched as he flicked his gaze down to it, and I knew he had not missed the fact the tip was still smeared with his own blood.

"Drive, or I will blind you," I said tightly.

"I cannot," Zak said again. "Please—I am much sorry."

The soldiers were only a few metres from us now, crabbing forwards. One carried an AK, pulled up hard into his shoulder, the other the SMG. They were younger than I'd first thought, probably only in their late teens, and they looked scared and excited in equal measure.

Firearms and bravado—never a good combination.

Surprisingly perhaps, it was Nils who took action. He lifted his booted foot over the centre console and stamped down on the Toyota's accelerator. Zak's feet had been covering the brake and clutch, but the shock of Nils's move and the instinctive fear of a man in sandals for having his toes mashed made him jerk them out of the way. The Toyota lurched forwards, engine revving into a loose-fanbelt squeal. Nils grabbed for the wheel.

The soldiers opened fire in reflex at the car's sudden move. Nils and Zak fought for control and neither of them won. The Toyota veered wildly towards the driver's side, striking the soldier with the SMG. He disappeared so fast under the front wheel he didn't have time to make a sound, the suspension bouncing sickeningly as the car rode up and over him. Then the front corner hit the rock face, and Nils's short-lived break for freedom came to an abrupt halt.

The other soldier raked the passenger side with fire. I heard the Swede cry out as I grabbed Alison by the collar of her shirt and punched open my door to bail out.

I found myself staring straight down into the wide-eyed

corpse of the soldier we'd just hit. The front tyre had rolled across his chest, forcing his insides out through every available orifice. Which was not, I judged, a pretty way to die.

On the bright side, the SMG he'd been holding was both accessible and intact. I snatched it up as I got out, ignoring the greasy stickiness on the strap, and forced the pair of us round the back of the Toyota.

"Keep your bloody head down," I growled to Alison, knowing that civilians—especially reporters—have a habit of wanting to gawk, thus turning themselves into very inviting targets.

The soldier who'd shot Nils had seen me get out and was expecting my head to pop up above the roof line, and that's where he was aiming. I took advantage of his distraction to lean out from behind the far rear tyre and put a three-round burst into his pelvis. He dropped, screaming.

The remaining pair of soldiers had initially hung back, only starting their run for us when the Toyota hit the rocks.

Laying down an accurate field of fire while sprinting towards a hostile target takes training and practice. They had neither. Still, there was always the chance of a lucky shot. I stayed low, braced on my elbows, and stitched across them as they ran, then rolled away.

The echo of blood and gunfire lifted slowly, leaving only a stark, static silence. I was aware of a low moaning from inside the car, the rasp of my own breath, and the hiss of steam from the Toyota's ruptured radiator. My eyes raked the landscape, looking for movement, threat. There was nothing. It all seemed to have happened in the space of a heartbeat.

You go into another zone in a firefight, one where normal morality is suspended, normal feelings of fear or revulsion are put aside. Sometimes it was hard to tell when everyday reality recommenced. Some soldiers never returned.

I swallowed a throatful of bile, starting to come back. My hands, gripping the SMG, were not quite steady. When I staggered to my feet, using the back end of the Toyota as a makeshift crutch, I found my legs were not quite steady either.

Four on one, and we survived—mostly. How the hell did that happen?

Alison took standing up as her cue to move, too. She scrambled up and dived back into the car, as if that might provide cover.

"Charlie, Nils is hurt!"

The soldier that had shot Nils was no longer screaming, I noted. He was no longer making any sound. I stepped over his body and yanked open the passenger door. Nils all but fell out into my arms. He'd taken a couple of AK rounds at close range in the arm and shoulder and had already managed to bleed enough to give the Toyota's front seat upholstery a colour change.

There was no arterial spray, which was a good thing. If we could patch him up long enough to get him across the border, and if he didn't go into shock first, Parker's people would take care of him from there.

The shoulder wound was a fairly straightforward hit. The 7.62mm round had smashed his collarbone and gone straight through the flimsy seat back to bury itself around where Alison and I had been crouching, before I'd pulled her out of the car.

Nils hadn't been so lucky with the second round. That looked to have entered his forearm at a shallow angle, ploughed a furrow into his flesh like a diving submarine, and exited, messily, through the back of his elbow. I was no orthopaedic surgeon, but one look was enough to tell me the lower part of his arm was completely screwed.

I retrieved the rudimentary first-aid kit and roll of duct tape from my holdall on the rear seat. Alison ripped open a couple of field dressings and I taped them in place. There wasn't much I could do with the arm except tape it back together and hope for the best. Duct tape is tough enough and waterproof enough to contain bleeding in an emergency. I wouldn't go anywhere without it.

Nils had blenched beneath his tan—any paler and we'd be able to see right through him. His skin had that waxy tint and he was panting around the pain, swearing in several different languages when he had the breath to do so. Shock was already setting in.

Alison used her scarf to fashion a sling, keeping his injured arm tied close to his body for support. I went and checked the Land Cruiser, found the keys were not in it. That meant going through the pockets of the dead men for the keys. Not a task I relished.

It did tell me part of the reason I'd been able to kill them, though. They were all young, without the toughened hands of professional soldiers. Only one had army-style boots on. I did not allow myself to dwell on it. I'd done what I had to.

I went back to the car. Alison had managed to get Nils out and was trying to persuade him to lie down to ease his depleted circulation, something he refused to do.

"Get him into the Land Cruiser," I told her. "We're leaving."

Alison looked at the bodies as if seeing them for the first time. "What about—?"

"Now, Alison."

I leaned into our wrecked car across Nils's empty seat and looked at Zak. He hadn't moved since the soldiers had opened fire on us, and I expected to find him dead, but his eye opened and swivelled slowly in my direction. His body was beyond still, it was immobile. I glanced down, saw the blood on the side of his clothing and realised he'd taken a stray round in the ribs that had probably lodged somewhere near his spine. He was paralysed.

"I am sorry," Zak said again, little more than a whisper.

"So am I," I said gravely. "Was it for money?"

Zak's face twitched into something that was more grimace than smile. "No," he said. "It was for my country. For honour, yes?" His gaze followed Alison and Nils as they stumbled across towards the other vehicle. "They will…ruin us."

———

I DIDN'T EXPECT to see Alison Cranmore again except on the news —and there I couldn't miss her. The dramatic—not to mention dramatised—story of how she and her intrepid cameraman had escaped from a war zone, pursued by all sides, was syndicated to every channel who would give it air time.

Alison looked good on camera, with a black-and-white *keffiyeh* slung casually around her neck, steady of eye and serious of voice. I was glad she didn't try to rope me into her personal media circus, and to begin with, she didn't.

Then about six weeks after the extraction, I got word she was asking for a meet. I had a London stopover on the way back from a job in Saudi, and—more out of curiosity than anything else—agreed to meet her in Soho House on the corner of Greek Street.

The once-seedy area was now filled with TV production companies and trendy wine bars where the movers and shakers of the arts world could not only be seen but heard as well.

The more things change…

It was summer in London and the city was wilting in the unaccustomed heat. It was a relief to climb the stairs to Soho House's upper-floor bar where the open windows allowed cross-flow ventilation.

I was early as a matter of course, but Alison was already there, having an intense discussion with a man I judged from his clothes and manner to be a TV producer of some kind. I sat at the bar nursing a tonic water until they were done. He gathered up his iPad and strode away with the air of a man who has far more important places to go and people to see.

"Sorry about that," Alison said, coming over. "Come and join me."

She looked fit and well, and far more relaxed than when I'd last seen her. She was dressed to blend with her surroundings, fashionable and expensive, her hair styled and nails shaped and polished. I'd just got off a long-haul flight and what felt like an equally long-haul taxi ride, and it showed.

We skated round the pleasantries while we ordered food and the waitress departed.

"I was hoping you might agree to an interview," Alison said then. "About your part in our escape."

A little late for that, isn't it?

"I can't," I said, trying to make a show of regret. "There's no way I can blend into the background well enough to do my job if you put me centre stage. I'm sorry."

She nodded, as if she'd half-expected that response, but it was something that had to be tried. "Well, at least let me buy you lunch—as a thank you."

I picked up my glass. "So, how's Nils?"

"Recovering well, as far as I know," she said, smiling now. "It's amazing what they can do with prosthetics these days. He's even talking about getting a camera built into his new arm."

"A pity Zak wasn't so lucky," I said.

The smile faded. "Excuse me?"

"Zak," I repeated. "There was nobody to medevac him off to a private Swiss clinic, so he had to rely on the local butchers. Infection got him in the end—took him about a fortnight to die."

"Oh...that's"—she searched for the right word—"sad," she came up with at last. "But he did lead us into a trap."

I looked at her. "So he deserved what he got, is that it?"

She flushed, but I didn't miss her sideways glance to check who might be listening in. She needn't have bothered—I was purposely keeping my voice down. For now.

"No, but you know what I mean. We could have been killed," she said, gaining confidence. "Nils lost an arm, for heaven's sake. You can't expect me to weep for someone who would do that."

"He did what he believed was right," I said. "It's the most any of us can do. The most any of us *should* do."

She stiffened. "What's that supposed to mean?"

"I thought you told Nils, outside that café, that you were there to report the news, not become a part of it."

Alison lifted an uncomfortable shoulder. "I *still* believe that," she said in a low voice.

I shook my head. "So, how did you end up as the next TV Dangerwoman, then?"

She grimaced. "Not my first choice, I admit, but I had to give them *something* to justify the expense of being out there."

I put my glass down, wiped a trickle of condensation from the side of it. "And what happened to your earth-shattering original story?"

Her face turned wry. "They squashed it."

I raised an eyebrow. "Who—your network?"

"Yes…well, not really." She started to shake her head, then stopped. "Pressure from above. They caved."

"Does that mean I'm never going to find out what that whole damn thing was all about?"

She hesitated, shifting awkwardly on the squashy sofa. The open window was to her left, the breeze stirring against her artfully casual hair. A motorbike with a raucous exhaust roared past in the street below. She looked a million miles away from the terrified and bloodied figure I'd pulled from that desert ambush.

"Well, I did sign a confidentiality agreement and—"

I leaned forwards, lowered my voice. "Aren't you people always banging on about the public's right to know? Don't you think at least that *I* have a right to know?"

Her shoulders came down. "Yes," she said at last. "Yes, you do." She took a deep swig of her drink, something in a tall glass with a lot of fruit salad—probably Pimm's—and set it down carefully on the low table in front of her. "We managed to get hold of some video from about a year ago—government archives," she said. "Amazing how often these tin-pot regimes record stuff like this for their own amusement. It showed the massacre of a group of dissidents. A big group of them. They were just herded into the desert and machine-gunned, for sport." Her face contorted at the memory. "The kind of thing you could only watch once, and that was once too many."

"Massacres happen all the time," I said calmly. "What was special about this one?"

She glanced at me in reproof. "The people behind the guns," she said. "The president himself was one of those pulling the trigger and laughing while he did so. We tracked down and interviewed some of the survivors, got their stories to intercut with the original footage. It was compelling and horrifying both at the same time."

There was a wistful note in her voice, though. Stories that were both compelling and horrifying were the ones that tended to win Pulitzers. Maybe that was her biggest regret.

I shrugged. "Sadly, that happens all the time, too."

She sighed, as if she'd been hoping that part of the tale might have been enough to satisfy me. The waitress arrived then with our salads, deposited them with a flourish and bustled away again. I let Alison pick at her food for a few moments, then nudged her to continue.

"What was special, Alison?"

She put down her fork. "One of the other people involved was the ex-deputy president," she said flatly.

That took a moment to penetrate. "Hang on—isn't he the one who denounced the president and broke away to lead the opposition—?"

"The one who's just routed the old regime and been sworn in as the new leader?" she said, a cynical note in her voice now. "The one the west is courting? That's him."

This was the man Zak had supported, the one he'd spoken of when he'd claimed to act in honour. *For my country.* He had wanted to kill the story, and the storytellers, to prevent the public disgrace of a disgraceful man. He'd given his life for that loyalty.

"They will ruin us," he'd said of Alison and Nils. Maybe it was better to have a strong dictator than a nation in chaos. Events in Iraq and Libya had proven that. Was it also worth the price in civil liberties? Somebody thought so—somebody high enough up to make it happen.

I glanced at her. "So, what was it all for—personal glory?"

Her face twitched. "It's never clear-cut, Charlie," she said. "It wasn't my first choice to make myself into the story, but I *had* to do something to justify the time and expense. I couldn't put the original story out, and I couldn't take it elsewhere—"

"Why not?" I interrupted. "Why couldn't you take it to another station, another network?"

"Because I have a contract that wouldn't let me do that," she said with the exaggerated patience of someone talking to a child. "And if I'd broken it, I might have been blacklisted, never got another job."

"Bollocks," I said shortly. "It might have delayed your next promotion, but it would have made your name as a journalist of principle."

She eyed me cynically. "I could have gone to jail."

"The same answer applies—possibly with a longer delay."

Alison let her breath out in an annoyed spurt, still looking past me, I noticed, to see who was paying attention to our quiet disagreement. "Charlie, that's simply not how things happen in the real world—"

"No, it damn well isn't," I shot back, low but harsh enough for her eyes to jump back to mine. "In the *real* world, Alison, I killed four men—little more than boys—to protect you and your bloody story. If you were never going to have the balls to use it, you could have left via the airport weeks before it all went bad and saved me the trouble." I let that settle for a moment, then added. "And Zak would still be alive, too."

"But he betrayed us."

"So you told the world," I agreed dryly, and the pink stain rose again above her collar. "But in the *real world* you're so fond of, Zak was the one who behaved with honour. Misguided perhaps, but honour of a kind nevertheless." I got to my feet, looked down at her for a long moment. "You were the one who betrayed, not just yourself, but everyone in that godforsaken country."

She flinched. "That's a low blow, Charlie."

"Is it?" I said. "Whatever happened to that old newspaper saying—'publish and be damned'? What happened to having the courage of your convictions?"

"There were consequences—not just for me!"

"There are always consequences, Alison," I said tiredly. "Sometimes the truth hurts like hell, but—trust me—it's nothing compared to the pain of a lie."

———

More to Read!

If you liked this, then you may also like the later Charlie Fox novels, where she is in full-blown professional bodyguard mode. Why not take a look at CHARLIE FOX: BODYGUARD eBoxset of books 4, 5, and 6? And please check out the rest of the series **here**, including ABSENCE OF LIGHT, book #11, which sees Charlie providing security for a rescue team after an earthquake.

6

ACROSS THE BROKEN LINE

THIS CHARLIE FOX short story was written especially for my newsletter members and it was a long time before it became more widely available. I always wanted to write something with a broken-up timeline, but my early attempts ended in frustration. Originally, I conceived this tale to be the final story in the FOX FIVE: A CHARLIE FOX SHORT STORY COLLECTION, but when it I couldn't get it as I wanted it, I shelved it, temporarily, and wrote something else instead.

As is always the way, though, the basic idea wouldn't leave me alone. Fortunately, I was able to write the bones of it and then put it aside for several months to ferment gently in the back of my mind. The time jumps, backwards and forwards from three weeks ago to right now, still proved a challenge, but also a great framework.

Here, Charlie is tasked to protect a principal on the run-up to the holiday season in New York City. Not everyone is going to get exactly what they wish for as a Christmas gift. Some, though, might just get what they deserve…

———

Fifteen minutes ago…

SHOVING a loaded gun in somebody's face is never going to make you friends but it certainly works for influencing people. The uniformed guy on the business end of my SIG Sauer P229 looked both unfriendly *and* influenced, that was for sure.

He froze halfway through bringing his own weapon clear of the holster on his hip. From what I could see of the hammer and the top of the slide it looked like a big Colt. A useful piece. I was glad he didn't get chance to finish the draw.

I couldn't blame the guy for trying, though. I'd just crashed a reinforced Lincoln Navigator through the security barrier he was supposed to be manning. That kind of thing tends to have that kind of effect.

Behind us was a huge warehouse, looming. Even by American standards, it was enormous—practically big enough to have its own motto and design of flag. It stood in rather sterile landscaped grounds, made bleaker by the unmarked covering of snow. The place was apparently deserted apart from the security post—and the slightly dented Navigator I'd just skid-parked by the main entrance.

"Where are they?" I demanded.

The security guard didn't answer, nor did he take his eyes off the gun in my hands, watching for his opportunity. Now I got a good look at him I saw he was at least six-four and probably two hundred and thirty pounds, most of it muscle. He also had the narrowed calm of previous armed contact—an ex-military man.

Just my luck.

"My name is Charlie Fox," I said, speaking clear and loud. "I'm the bodyguard."

Something of that went in. I saw a flicker of understanding. I took a calculated risk, brought the SIG's front sight up off target and uncurled my finger from the trigger. His shoulders dropped slightly in relief. Mine probably did the same.

"Mrs Duvall left strict instructions," he said then, brusque with residual tension. "No interruptions. Not for anything."

"Well, you might say Mrs Duvall was under duress."

He nodded, still wary. "Mr D—her husband—he went in 'bout a quarter hour before she arrived," he said, as if that confirmed it.

Shit.

So much for risking my neck on the snow-slicked roads

trying to get here ahead of them. New York in the winter can be a bitch.

"Call the cops," I said, starting for the entrance to the building.

The guy moved as if to block me. "Hey, you can't go in there!"

"If I don't, one of them will be coming out in a body bag," I said. "Your choice."

He hesitated as if I might be overstating it, saw from my face that I was not.

"You don't understand," he said, waving an arm towards the warehouse. "This whole place is fully automated—state of the art. The motorised stock-retrieval system moves pretty damned fast. No way can you go in there unless they shut it down. You'll get yourself killed."

"Well, that's *my* choice." I threw the security guard a last look over my shoulder. Tall and powerful, with a neck that cried out for a bolt through it, his hand resting on the butt of the Colt in reflex. "Be sure to tell them you tried to stop me."

———

A week ago...

"Ah, Charlie, come on in. This is Olivia Duvall," Parker said. "Ms Duvall has just engaged our services. You'll be looking after her."

An elegant, dark-haired woman rose from one of the client chairs in Parker Armstrong's office, turning as I shut the door and came forwards. She was wearing designer sunglasses, but I saw from the angle of her head that she gave me the usual once-over. There was a momentary hesitation while she compared her mental expectation of a female bodyguard with the reality. I'm not built like a member of the Bulgarian ladies' Olympic weightlifting team, so I rarely match up. I was used to that.

She probably wasn't quite what I expected either.

I held out my hand and we shook. Olivia Duvall came roughly up to my nose, which was saying something because I wasn't exactly supermodel-tall myself. She was carefully put together and neat as a miniature doll. Classy suit over a high-neck blouse—style that had been hard won rather than inbred. She had a firm grip, seemed vaguely disappointed when I didn't grind her bones into dust in return.

"If I *looked* like a bodyguard," I said mildly, reading her thoughts, "I wouldn't be much use to you." A standard reply. One I'd found myself compelled to use many times before.

She paused, then gave me a somewhat tremulous smile. "Ah…no, of course not." But she looked in my boss's direction while she said it.

"Charlie's one of my best operatives," Parker said. "She'll take good care of you."

Olivia did not necessarily look reassured but she sank back into her chair. I sat opposite, unbuttoning my jacket so the gun behind my right hip didn't pull it out of line.

Parker looked at the woman opposite as if for permission to expand. She lifted her shoulder a fraction.

"Ms Duvall is having a little trouble with her husband—"

"A *little*? Try a *lot*! The bastard tried to kill me." Olivia stopped, took a shaky breath and let her gaze drop to the hands clasped tightly in her lap. "I still can't believe Joe would do that to me—to *us*. Not after all these years."

"What happened?"

"Ms Duvall is seeking to dissolve her marriage," Parker said, his voice dry and cool, offering no judgements. "She believes her husband may have a more…permanent solution in mind."

Olivia's head came up sharply, as if hoping to catch an expression of disbelief. Almost defiant, she reached up and removed the sunglasses. Worn indoors I'd thought them to be an affectation. They were not.

Beneath the tinted lenses, the whites of her eyes were streaked with red.

"He tried to smother me with a pillow two nights ago," she said, her voice flat. "I woke up with it over my face. I couldn't breathe, I just went crazy, managed to get my head turned so I could get some air." She gave us both a defiant glare, as if we'd doubt she was capable.

I looked at her hands. They were small and narrow, nails painted a delicate coral pink. Not the kind of hands you could imagine successfully fighting off a larger, stronger attacker.

Parker glanced at me, still nothing in his voice. "Ms Duvall's two children were asleep in the house at the time," he said.

I raised my eyebrows. "Has your husband ever behaved violently towards your children?"

She hesitated. "No," she said quietly. "At least…not yet."

And there it was—out, stark and edgy.

Voiced.

Every mother's nightmare. The reason she had sought out the kind of protection offered by someone like Parker. By someone like me.

"Did he offer any excuse—try to explain?" Parker asked.

Olivia shot him an old-fashioned look, as if only a man could ask such a question, and directed her answer to me. "I–I must have passed out for a second. When I came to, got my breath and shoved the pillow off of me, the bastard was standing in the bathroom doorway, pretending like nothing had happened and asking what all the noise was about," she said, her voice neutral almost to the point of detachment.

I glanced at Parker. "I get the impression this wasn't an isolated incident."

There was another fractional pause. "As I was leaving the office, about six weeks ago, someone tried to run me down," she admitted. "I didn't get a look at the driver—it was dark—but it was the same make and model as Joe's truck. And when I got home he was in his workshop, said he hadn't left the house all afternoon."

There was something in her face. "But?"

"The hood of his truck was still warm."

"Had he any previous history of violence?"

She didn't shake her head right away, as if loyalty were over-coming truth. "Joe was in the military for a while," she admitted. "He was discharged. Doesn't like to talk about it much, but— with the kind of training they get—well, I always wondered…"

…*if it turned him into a killer.*

"And what has he done since then?"

A flicker of annoyance crossed her features. At the question or the coming answer, I wasn't sure.

"For work, you mean? He doesn't *do* anything. After he shipped home he worked the mill for a while, like his daddy before him—'til they laid him off. Could hardly seem to get a job after that and when he did he couldn't seem to keep it." She was trying not to condemn—just not too hard. "Eventually, it was just easier all round for me to go out and find work, and that's what I did."

I checked out the designer suit, the matching accessories, the flash of jewellery at ears and wrists and fingers. The work Olivia Duvall had found clearly did not involve scrubbing floors. It seemed to surprise her that my face was blank.

"Ms Duvall has enjoyed no small measure of success," Parker said, and I heard the dry understatement.

She sighed, shifted in her seat. "I started up an online home-electronics company right out of my kitchen," she said with the matter-of-fact tone of someone who's recited this story many times. "I studied the market and simply…supplied that demand—straight from the manufacturer. No stock, no overheads."

"Ms Duvall is being modest," Parker said blandly. "She now controls one of the largest warehouse and distribution networks in the United States. I believe her turnover last year was well into eight figures."

"So, I assume—should you divorce—that Mr Duvall's current lifestyle would be somewhat adversely affected?" I said, matching my tone to Parker's.

Her mouth twitched again. "End of the line for the gravy train, you mean? Oh yeah." She paused again, uncomfortable. "His name isn't Duvall, by the way, it's Dabrowski—Josef Dabrowski."

I nodded without asking awkward questions, watched her face relax a little in response.

"You could go to the cops—get a restraining order."

She shook her head. "I have a high profile," she said, like that fact embarrassed her rather than being the peak for which she'd strived. "It would be all over the tabloids before the ink was dry on the paperwork."

Parker cleared his throat, "There are other steps—"

"Getting a gun, you mean?" Olivia interrupted. "I already did that. But the boys are at an age where they're fascinated by anything that goes bang. I have to keep the damn thing locked up so tight I'd never get to it before Joe—"

She broke off, drew in a long shaky breath. "I'm scared," she said, something in her voice that might have been reluctance to admit such a personal failing. "For me and for my kids. It's not just the money thing with Joe. He's always been so jealous… possessive. Even if he gives me a divorce, I know I'll be looking over my shoulder for the rest of my life. Unless…"

Her voice drifted away into a heavy silence, eyes still on her own whitened knuckles, and Parker's eyes flicked to mine. I caught acquiescence in their cool grey depths.

"We may be able to help you with that," I said and watched her head come up as if jerked on a wire. I rose, made sure she got a glimpse of the SIG on my hip. Not locked away tight to keep it out of the hands of children, but ready, instant. "We may be able to find a more…*permanent* solution of our own."

She allowed the hope to creep into her face, her cheeks flushing with a kind of guilty relief. "I just want to feel safe," she said at last. Evasive, but as close to tacit approval as we were likely to get.

I looked her straight in the eye, unblinking. "Don't worry," I said. "When I sign on to protect a principal, I'll die before I let any harm come to them."

———

Ten minutes ago…

"Olivia!"

My voice bounced off the stacks of electronics stretching up to the vast roof above like skyscrapers in an enclosed city.

I jogged along one of the main north-south aisles, past what appeared to be crated-up washing machines and refrigerators. Everything was swathed in enough plastic and polystyrene packaging to pollute a small ocean. Or a large one, come to that.

No doubt in an effort to save on running costs the lighting inside the warehouse was dim, but there was no staff to complain. The whole place was empty like an abandoned ship. I expected the floor to start listing at any moment as the vessel began her final dive for the seabed.

A faint squeaking noise behind me had me turning fast, the SIG in my hands, only to find a mechanical monster bearing down on me, two giant blades aiming for my stomach.

I leapt clear, flattening against the nearest racking. The unmanned electric forklift glided past oblivious, its electric motor almost silent. Only the sound of the rubber tyres on the painted concrete floor had warned me of its approach. As I watched, heart bumping against my ribs, the forklift stopped precisely level with a stack of steam ovens and began to tele- scope upwards to fulfil its pre-programmed instructions. I eyed the twin blades as they rose.

"Christ," I muttered under my breath. "Who designed this place—Freddy Krueger?"

The security guard's warning came back to me in a rush. Clearly, he had not been exaggerating the dangers.

The buzz of my cellphone in my inside jacket pocket nearly had me jumping out of my skin. I fumbled for it, left-handed, saw Parker's name on the display and almost dismissed the call. Almost.

Instead, I flipped the phone open, said tightly, "Not a good time."

"I realise that," my boss said dryly. "But this changes everything…"

———

Three weeks ago…

"I THINK my wife is maybe trying to get rid of me."

Josef Dabrowski had once been a handsome man, but time had not been kind to him. He was well over six feet, broad shoul- dered and narrow hipped but with a belly just starting to over- hang his belt. His fair hair was thinning backwards and his blue eyes were bagged beneath and crowded with laughter lines at the sides. He wore an old T-shirt and denims faded from too many rounds with the washing machine rather than designer stressing.

At a casual glance, I would have taken him for an out-of-work actor who'd just been to a casting call for construction workers. The too-clean hands gave him away.

Dabrowski certainly did not look at home in the living room of this mock Tudor mansion in a leafy suburb of New York unless he was there to quote for renovations.

He perched on the edge of a buttoned leather sofa, one of a matching pair that framed the ornate fireplace. There was a thick earthenware mug of coffee on the delicate table in front of his clasped hands. It seemed as out of place as he did in the elegant surroundings.

Opposite sat Parker Armstrong, slender by comparison and younger looking despite the prematurely grey hair. He was apparently relaxed, one arm draped along the low back of the sofa. A convincing illusion.

I stood to one side where I could see out of the front window along the driveway, just in case of visitors. Dabrowski had said he wasn't expecting anyone. We didn't like to take that for granted.

"Why not go to the cops?" It was Parker's standard opening question, and how people answered—or evaded—usually told him plenty.

"Go to the cops with what?" Dabrowski asked now, his voice bitter. "'Sides, my Olive is already prepping me as the bad guy."

"How?"

Alongside him, vibrating with a kind of righteous anger, was Bill Rendelson. I would have described him as Parker's right-hand man, except I knew Rendelson would take great offence at the remark. He'd lost his right arm to the shoulder in a parcel-bomb attack on the principal he'd been protecting some years previously. He made up for the loss by ruling the office with an iron fist, and seemed to nurture a deep resentment for those of us still active in the field.

Dabrowski shifted restlessly, making the leather squeak

beneath him. It was left to Rendelson to jump in, which he did with barely concealed impatience even towards his boss.

"Acting in public like she's real nervous of Joe, when he's never laid a hand on her," he growled. His eyes drifted over me. "However much she had it coming."

Dabrowski murmured a protest, automatic rather than heart-felt. "Hey, come on, Bill. *Someone* tried to run her down in my truck—it just wasn't *me* behind the wheel."

"You only got her word for that, Joe." Rendelson's tone was quiet but final. "No witnesses and it all happened where there just so happened to be no security cameras. Convenient, huh?"

Dabrowski opened his mouth then shut it again, whatever he was about to say interrupted by a fair-haired boy, possibly just into his teens, who catapulted into the living room doorway.

"Hey, Dad, tell Adam it's my turn! He won't—"

"Not now, Tanner," Dabrowski said, more heavy than sharp. "I got people here. Later, OK?"

Tanner looked downcast. "Adam *always* gets what he wants," he complained. "It's *so* not fair."

As if in victory, a burst of loud distorted music thundered down the stairs from the upper floor.

"Excuse me," Dabrowski muttered, rising. He stepped around Tanner, stood in the open doorway and yelled upwards, "Adam, turn that noise down! And play nice with your brother."

There was brief silence before the music returned, this time with a booming rap overlay:

"Ad-Ad-Adam. T-t-t-urn that noise d-d-down. Noise down. And play nice. Playnice, playniceplaynice—"

"ADAM!" Dabrowski roared, army in his voice now. "Turn it down right now or every last scrap of that gear goes on eBay in the morning. You hear me?"

The music cut off in mid-note. Dabrowski waited a moment longer, then nodded and headed back to his seat.

"Wouldn't happen if'n I had my own stuff," Tanner muttered as his father passed.

"Wait and see what Santa Claus brings you," Dabrowski replied. It sounded like an automatic response to an oft-made request.

His younger son rolled his eyes behind his father's back, then saw me watching and gave a sly grin. I kept my expression stony. I've never been exactly maternal but sneaky kids are the worst kind. Undeterred, he disappeared and shortly after came the pound of teenage feet up the stairs.

Dabrowski shrugged helplessly to Parker. "Boys, huh?"

"How old are they?"

"Tanner just turned thirteen," Dabrowski said. "Adam was sixteen last fall. I guess he's starting to find his younger brother a drag."

From what I'd just seen of Dabrowski junior, I couldn't blame the older brother for that.

"If your wife wants out," I said mildly, getting us back on track, "then surely a divorce would be easier?"

Rendelson gave a snort that might have been twisted laughter. With him, it was difficult to tell. "Not when you're on the rich list," he said.

He gave an abrupt twitch of his right shoulder, the kind that might once have resulted in the dismissive flick of a hand. I tracked the direction, saw a framed picture on the wall just behind a grand piano that had the look of furniture rather than an instrument.

I stepped closer, recognised it as a front cover of *Forbes*—the money mag. I unhooked the picture and carried it across to Parker.

The cover photo was of a woman standing with one fist on her hip, the other holding the hand of the boy who'd just ratted out his older brother. Adam stood a little way back from his mother and Tanner, both kids scrubbed up and shiny. The perfect family.

The headline read:

'OLIVIA DUVALL—SELF-MADE MILLIONAIRE SUPER-MOM'

"Ah," I murmured as I handed it to my boss. "You're married to *that* Olivia Duvall."

Dabrowski hesitated a moment, then nodded, as if caution on

the subject had become a habit hard to break. "She done good," he said, his voice a mix of shame and pride.

"So, she doesn't use the name Dabrowski?"

"Not anymore—something to do with 'brand image' or something." He shook his head. "She did explain it to me one time but…" He glanced at the pair of us briefly, a shy smile on his face. "I didn't take it in much. She calls herself Olivia now, not Olive. Don't like it when I tell folks it ain't so."

I looked for malice, saw only a hurt bewilderment. He looked for all the world like a man who was still in love with his wife, but she had reinvented herself. The woman he'd married didn't exist anymore.

"I'm guessing there was no prenup agreement," I said dryly. "So a divorce would cost Ms Duvall big bucks."

Dabrowski's face took on a stubborn cast. "She worked hard for what she's got. I only want what's fair and no more."

I heard his unspoken *"but"* and queried it.

"She knows I'd never let go of my boys," he said simply. "I raised 'em single-handed, near as dammit. Ever since I got laid off and my Olive set up on her own. Internet stuff." He spread hands so big he could have scooped up a litter of puppies in them, and jerked his head in the direction of upstairs. "Truth be told, the boys probably understand it better than I do."

"They're fine boys," Parker said, his eyes still on the picture.

Dabrowski ducked his head in acknowledgement. "We didn't always have money," he said. "Might be that way again—this economy, who knows? I've tried to keep their feet on the ground. They still do their chores, earn their allowance. I want to see 'em raised right."

"You could come to some arrangement over joint custody," Parker suggested.

"My Olive's an all-or-nothing kinda girl—always was," Dabrowski said. "I guess that's why she's done what she's done."

For a moment I thought he was referring to her business empire. It was left to Bill Rendelson to expand.

"She rigged his truck to explode."

I didn't respond to that immediately. It seemed a little outrageous, put baldly like that. And where would a middle-class suburban mother-of-two get the components for…?

"Ah," I realised, almost to myself, "she just happens to run an electronics company."

Bill Rendelson flicked me a brief look of surprise as if he hadn't expected me to put it together.

"It was kind of obvious to be a serious attempt," Dabrowski said quickly, like that excused the whole thing. When Parker raised an eyebrow, he shrugged. "I seen a lot of IEDs back when I was in the military."

"She really wants the boys that badly?" Parker asked.

"She's built her whole image on being some kind of super-mom," Rendelson said, twisting the words with contempt, "but she barely sees the kids from one day to the next. She just hates to lose."

"So you think getting rid of Joe might be a cheaper option for her," I said.

Rendelson began to bristle. "If it's the money you're so damn worried about, *I'll* pay the agency's going rate myself—"

"I'll pay what I can," Dabrowski said stoutly. "I ain't asking for charity."

Parker paused, considering. Bill Rendelson leaned in, as if about to plead and loath to have to do it in front of me, muttered, "Joe and I served together. I don't often ask for personal favours, boss…"

Parker got to his feet, buttoning his jacket, and it might have been my imagination but his gaze lingered over the two kids in the photograph. "Let's worry about the money later," he said. "Mr Dabrowski, we offer a very special service in cases like this. Not just close protection in the traditional sense, but a more… proactive approach."

I saw the man's frown at the sideways terminology and simplified it. "What he means is, we draw out the threat and neutralise it."

Dabrowski rose also, suddenly uneasy. He was half a head taller than Parker, and towered over both me and Rendelson.

"I just need to know I'm gonna be around for my boys," he said again.

"I think we can arrange that."

"Yeah? How?"

I smiled. Was it really only three weeks ago? It seemed so easy then.

"By offering to help your wife."

———

Five minutes ago…

"OLIVIA!" I called again. "We need to get out of here before we all get killed."

"Isn't that what you want?" her voice yelled back. The echoes made it harder to define direction. But at least she was talking to me.

I skirted the forklift as it began to retract, balancing a pallet-load of HD flatscreen TVs. I watched it whirr away quietly into the gloom.

"Things have changed," I said. I crabbed forwards with great care, keeping close to the stacks. "Whatever's happening here, it's not what you think."

"Oh really?" There was a harsh bark of laughter. "What made you betray me, Charlie? Did he promise you a fat bonus if I didn't make it to the final decree? Well, I got news for you, honey. Anything happens to me, every cent goes to the boys." Her voice caught audibly. "If the bastard hasn't killed them already."

My ears finally got a fix. I dived through one of the cross-streets—there was no other way to describe the gaps between the racking. One up and two across.

And there she was, staring around her with fear-filled eyes. She was clutching the little revolver she'd bought for her own protection after claiming her husband tried to kill her. I moved into view with the SIG up and levelled.

"Put it down, Olivia," I said, loud enough for there to be no mistake, soft enough not to startle her into a negligent discharge.

She spun with a gasp, even so, staring at me. If I expected to find her dishevelled I was disappointed. She still looked like she'd stepped out of the pages of a fashion mag.

"Not while that bastard's out there," she said. She gestured to the SIG. "What—are you really going to shoot me?"

"No," said another voice, deep and bitter. Joe Dabrowski came rushing out of the shadows with his own gun raised and pointed straight at his wife. "But I will."

And then, out of nowhere, the darkness came whistling in on us and Dabrowski's hand jerked.

He fired.

———

An hour ago…

"THE BOMB WAS A BLIND," Parker said.

I felt the Navigator twitch slightly as I reacted to the news. I almost dropped my cellphone—which served me right for not taking his call on hands-free while I was driving. It had begun to snow again and the roads were lethal, even with four-wheel drive.

"Charlie—you still there?"

"Yeah, I'm still here," I said. "What do you mean, it was a blind?"

"It was too complex for an amateur to have put together. Olivia Duvall may run an electronics company, but that doesn't mean she has the knowledge on how to build an improvised device, so I had Bill check it out. We've been waiting for his tame IED expert to rotate home from Afghanistan and he's gotten an expert opinion—she couldn't have done it."

"Come on, Parker, any school kid with an internet connection can find out how to build an improvised device in about twenty minutes."

"True," he allowed, "but you've been alongside her twenty-four/seven for the past week—when does she have the time?"

"It's like anything—you want it badly enough, you *make* the time." But even as I said it, I realised that Olivia Duvall ran to the kind of schedule that would make presidents and prime ministers wilt.

"So, what are we saying?" I demanded. "That she had help?"

"Or that Dabrowski put the thing together himself," Parker said flatly. I could almost hear Bill Rendelson simmering in the background. "He did admit to having extensive experience during his time with the military."

"But if Joe built the bomb he claimed his wife used to try to kill him does that mean—?" I began.

"That we've been taken for a ride?" Parker finished for me. "I hope not." His voice was grim. "Where are you?"

"On my way to meet Olivia at the house."

"What's your ETA?"

I took the phone away from my ear just long enough to use both hands on the Navigator's wheel. I swung the big vehicle through a gap in the dirty banks of ploughed snow and into the tree-lined driveway. "I'm there now," I said. The house came visible through the sparse foliage. I glanced across, saw the front door standing slightly ajar. "I'll call you back."

For once I didn't bother taking the Navigator round to the side of the building to the tradesman's entrance. I left it sprawled untidily on the cleared stone setts of the driveway and ran to the doorway, sliding the SIG from its holster as I went.

Taking a deep breath, I nudged the heavy oak door open with the toe of my boot and slipped inside fast. Nobody fired at me while I was silhouetted in the opening. A good sign.

I went from room to room, moving quickly, quietly. The place had been festooned with Christmas decorations since my visit with Parker and Bill Rendelson, and the living room smelled of pine from the eight-foot tree near the grand piano. The time of seasonal ill-will was rampantly upon us.

But I found nothing out of place—except the people. There was nobody at home.

It was a Saturday, late morning. Joe Dabrowski should have been there with the boys. Olivia had said she wouldn't be working for once. They had planned a family brunch, but when I stuck my head into the kitchen everything was squared away. There were no signs of food preparation.

I looked into Joe's workshop, which was empty and unlit. Tanner's room was its usual muddle, scattered with dirty clothes that Olivia refused to allow the cleaning service to pick up for him.

The room of the older boy, Adam, was neater, just cluttered with his music paraphernalia, the latest piece of which he'd bought second-hand from eBay. Joe had told me that the kid had bitched about the fact that Olivia sold all the latest gear through her company, but wouldn't give him more than staff discount. They were trying to teach him the value of things. It was taking a while to sink in.

I went back downstairs and stuck my head into Olivia's study. Her handbag and briefcase were both sitting on the desktop. If the open front door had sounded the first note of alarm, that sent it up a notch. Olivia never went anywhere without her cellphone, laptop, and diary. To find them apparently abandoned was worrying.

I scanned the desktop, saw the message light blinking on the answering machine. Suddenly wary, I used the butt of the SIG to tap the replay button.

"Hey, Olivia." Joe's voice came raspy and barely recognisable out of the tinny speaker. "I've got the boys. Unless you want to be burying them, you'll ditch the bodyguard and meet me at that mausoleum you call your empire. And you better hurry."

"Shit," I muttered under my breath. I punched the redial button on my cellphone. While it rang out, I paused the message, set it to replay. "Hey Parker," I said. "I think you—and Bill— need to hear this…"

―――――

Now…

THE MOTORISED FORKLIFT caught Joe Dabrowski little more a glancing blow. Even so, I heard the bones of his shoulder give way like an old dry branch as it flung him out and to the side. If he hadn't heard that betraying squeak at the last moment, started to turn, it would have mowed him flat.

As it was, at least the shock of it deflected his aim enough to go wide. The discharge was still brutal in the echoing cavern, then the gun was falling from his grasp.

I darted forwards and kicked the weapon out of his reach. It was an old Beretta, a standard military sidearm, something that was no doubt familiar to him.

I scooped one hand under his good arm and dragged him back against the stacks just in case another forklift bore down on us. He slumped there, breathing hard. The shock was taking care of the pain—for now. He was grey with it.

I turned back, to find Olivia Duvall was covering both of us with the little revolver.

Give me strength.

"Olivia," I said sharply. "Put that down before you hurt yourself—or I have to do it for you."

"Damn right she'll hurt you," Dabrowski told his wife through gritted teeth. "And she'll keep hurting you until you tell us what you've done with my boys."

"What *I've* done?" Olivia demanded. "It's *you* who's threatening to bury them, you bastard!"

I said calmly, "Olivia, we can sort this out, but not here and not at gunpoint." And to prove it I slid the SIG away, ignoring Dabrowski's groan. I held out my hand towards her, palm out.

She wavered for a moment, then I saw the determined glint come into her eyes.

"Not until—"

"Look out!" I yelled, and rushed her.

There was no incoming forklift this time, but the possibility was real enough to make her look. As she did so I rammed my elbow into the fleshy vee just below her ribcage. It knocked the stuffing out of her just as effectively.

By the time she'd recovered enough to curse me, I'd spun the cylinder of the little revolver and dropped the live rounds out into my pocket.

And then another forklift *did* come whooshing out of the murky darkness. We stepped back quickly.

"Now you've temporarily finished trying to kill each other," I muttered, "can we please get out of here before we all qualify for the Darwin Awards by removing ourselves from the gene pool in the most inventive way possible?"

After the dimness of the warehouse interior, it seemed unnaturally bright outside, sunlight gleaming from the pristine snow around the exterior. I blinked a few times and saw Parker waiting with the security guard, standing by another of the company Lincoln Navigators.

The two boys, Adam and Tanner, slouched between them. They looked like they'd rather be anywhere else.

Their parents both stopped dead. Dabrowski tried to wipe his forehead, suddenly realising his arm didn't work properly. He stared at it like he couldn't for the life of him work out when that happened.

His eyes, when they turned to me, were bewildered. "But—?"

"Let me guess, Joe," I said gently. "You got a message, apparently from your wife, telling you she had the boys and unless you wanted to arrange their funerals, you'd meet her here."

Dabrowski's brow furrowed. "How the hell—?"

"Olivia got the same message," I said. "From you."

Olivia's attention finally tore away from her sons and towards me. "What?"

"You were set up—both of you," I said. "I had a phone call from Parker inside to confirm it. He analysed the messages. Your voices were sampled and digitally manipulated. They could have made it sound like you were saying anything."

"But…" Olivia stumbled into silence. "How…?"

"The 'how' is the easy part," I said. "It's the 'who' you're not going to like."

They had moved instinctively closer to each other, I noticed. Which was possibly a good sign.

"That can't—" The look Olivia threw me was fast and vicious. "You've crossed the line, Charlie."

"Trust me," I said. "That line was already broken."

And despite the fact it was Olivia who'd had the drive and intelligence to start a major business from the ground up, it was Joe who put it together first.

"Adam has one of those electronic synthesisers," he said

slowly. "He was always recording our voices—even made it sound like I could sing."

"No, no," Olivia said, shaking her head as if that would make it all go away. "But...someone tried to smother me..." She put a hand to her throat. "No, not Adam! That's ridiculous! I'm his mother—"

"No offence," I said, "but if someone the size and weight of your husband wanted to suffocate you, you'd be dead."

"And the bomb?" Joe asked, sounding hollow.

"Olivia hasn't the time or the expertise to put have put it together," I said, "but the average teenager, spending hours on the internet, and with access to your workshop at the house, could have something of that level of sophistication constructed in a couple of hours. Particularly," I added, "if their father just so happened to have spent time dismantling IEDs after Desert Storm, and told them a few war stories."

For a moment they both stood there, then Olivia said in little more than a whisper. "Adam was learning to drive your truck, Joe—ever since he got his learner's permit."

They both turned, in unison, and looked at their children again. Only this time their gaze was very different.

Adam gave his younger brother a vicious jab in the arm. "I *told* you," he complained.

Tanner's cheeks were burning. "Adam, shut *up*!"

I began to change my mind about which of them had been the ringleader in this enterprise.

The security guard calmly pulled them apart before they could come to further blows. I handed Parker the weaponry I'd collected from husband and wife.

"Good work, Charlie," he said.

"Same to you, boss," I said. "If Bill hadn't analysed those tapes so fast, we'd be scraping bodies out of there right now." I thought of my own near-miss with the forklift. "Probably mine included."

Olivia Duvall was looking almost as shocked as her husband. He put his good arm around his wife and for what I imagined was the first time in months, she didn't pull away from such a public embrace.

"Why?" she murmured then. She cleared her throat, gave her sons a piercing stare. "Why the hell would either of you want us dead…? I mean, *why*, for God's sake?"

Their answer was sullen silence. I glanced back at their parents. They'd been prepared to fight over custody of their ungrateful children in the divorce. Maybe now the fight would be to see who *didn't* have to put up with them.

I shrugged. "You gave the reason yourself, Olivia. 'If anything happens to me,' you said, 'every cent goes to the boys.' Maybe they just wanted Christmas to come early this year."

———

More to Read!

If you liked this, then you may also like the later Charlie Fox novels, where she is in full-blown professional bodyguard mode. Why not take a look at CHARLIE FOX: BODYGUARD eBoxset of books 4, 5, and 6? And please check out the rest of the series **here**, including THIRD STRIKE, where Charlie has to face the nightmare of protecting her own parents. (Much as, some of the time, she'd be first in line to shoot them…)

7

KILL ME AGAIN SLOWLY

THIS CHARLIE FOX short story was written especially for MURDER UNDER THE OAKS, an anthology of short stories edited by Art Taylor, which was published to coincide with the Bouchercon World Mystery Convention 2015 in Raleigh, North Carolina, where I was privileged to be one of the two International Guests of Honour.

I wanted to write something that had a strong link to North Carolina, and at the same time put Charlie in a situation she had never before experienced.

This idea was one that had been hanging around in the back of my mind as a possible full-blown futuristic science-fiction novel for some time, but I suddenly realised it could work for her. And it was one of the few ways I could involve Charlie in events that would otherwise be impossible.

But if you want to know how, you'll just have to read on!

I am proud to report that MURDER UNDER THE OAKS won the Anthony Award 2016 for the Best Anthology/Short Story Collection.

————

I KNEW something was wrong when the waiter arrived before the punch-line. Up till that point, things had been going well.

Bizarrely, it has to be said, but well.

I was sitting at a table for six in *Rick's Café Américain* in

Casablanca. The dry southeasterly wind, the *Chergui,* pushed gently across Morocco from the Sahara, adding a warm lilt to the evening.

On the café stage, Glenn Miller led the jazz band with Wynton Marsalis giving it his all in a trumpet solo. I had to look twice to recognise a down-dressed Elton John at the piano.

The place was packed with beautiful people in immaculate clothes, a mix of uniforms and evening dress. All of them were having the time of their lives. Nobody was raucously drunk, nobody sent back their plate to the kitchen, and for once the haze of smoke that hung beneath the vaulted ceiling did not get right up my nose.

Best of all, nobody was paying too much attention to the other people at my table.

To my left, Oscar Wilde lounged elegantly in his chair. Next to him was Marilyn Monroe, while further round sat Groucho Marx and Dorothy Parker. And directly on my right, next to Mrs Parker, the final player in our little sextet was my host, Asher Campbell Cooper III.

He was dressed in a white tuxedo jacket, snowy white shirt, black pants and a bow tie that was just imperfect enough to be perfect. He looked about thirty, wide of shoulder and narrow of hip, with startling blue eyes and long tanned fingers that toyed with the stem of his champagne flute as he launched almost diffidently into the joke he never got to finish.

At that point, his audience was listening with absolute attention. I caught the curve of Dorothy Parker's lips in what appeared to be genuine amusement. Even Oscar Wilde's languid pose had stilled, his brow creasing with the effort of searching fruitlessly for a witty retort to follow.

"So the three nuns, the Russian drug dealer and the clown are being pursued through the food hall of Harrods by the Japanese ABBA tribute band, when the clown's cellphone rings—"

The waiter, Emile, materialised at Asher's shoulder and cleared his throat.

"Excuse me, sir," he said, bowing slightly, "but there is a telephone call for you. The party pressed upon me to convey that it was most urgent."

Asher shut his open mouth, sighed heavily and flicked me a glance.

"See?" he demanded, buttoning his jacket as he rose. "If you'll excuse me, ladies and gentlemen? I'll be back to finish my story momentarily."

"This suspense is terrible," Oscar Wilde drawled. "I hope it will last."

Groucho Marx waved his cigar expansively, reached around the beaded lamp in the centre of the table for the champagne bottle and offered to top up Dorothy Parker's glass. She shook her head.

"One more drink and I'll be under the host."

I stood also, fell into step alongside Asher as Emile shepherded us through the crowded tables towards the bar. On it, I could see an old-fashioned black telephone with the receiver off the hook.

"Is this how it usually starts?" I asked.

Asher nodded. "Or something similar. Damn shame. That's my best joke."

"There'll be another time."

Next to the bar was a narrow curtained doorway. As we passed I flicked the curtain aside. Nobody lurked behind it.

Asher grinned at me over his shoulder as he reached for the receiver. "You packing?"

I spread my arms to indicate my strapless, backless, practically arseless dress—his choice, not mine. "And where, exactly, did you expect me to hide a piece in this outfit?" I shot up a splayed hand before he could respond. "No, don't answer that."

He was still smiling as he picked up the phone. It didn't last.

"Yeah, thanks Brant but I'd kinda guessed as much," he said and slammed the receiver back onto its cradle.

"Trouble?"

"Uh-huh. Brant's rounding up the usual suspects."

As we weaved back towards our table, I murmured into his ear, "If it all goes bad, you know what to do."

"Yes, ma'am."

I let my gaze wash across the patrons, the staff, and the musicians. Nobody was watching us too closely, or trying too hard to avoid doing so. Nobody's attitude had changed. But I was only too aware that I was in a situation where nothing could be trusted.

"If you want to know what God thinks of money," Dorothy Parker was saying to the table at large as Asher politely handed me into my seat, "just look at the people he gave it to."

Marilyn Monroe gave a breathy giggle and said, "Oh, I don't want to make money, I just want to be wonderful."

Dorothy Parker rolled her eyes.

Airily sipping his champagne, Oscar Wilde said, "Who, being loved, is poor?"

Groucho Marx rested his elbow on the table, his chin on his cupped palm, and gazed at Marilyn Monroe. "Marry me and I'll never look at another horse."

"Oh!" Marilyn Monroe glared at him, threw down her serviette and leaped to her feet. "Respect is one of life's greatest treasures." Her eyes were bright with unshed tears. "I mean, what does it all add up to if you don't have that?"

She leaned down for her purse, but when she straightened there was a bolo machete with an eighteen-inch blade in her right hand and she held it like it wasn't her first time. With an inarticulate war cry, she used her chair as a springboard to launch herself across the table aiming straight for Asher's head.

What the…?

Hurling myself sideways I sent him, chair and all, sprawling backwards. The slashing arc of what should have been a deadly blow sizzled the air where Asher's throat had been only moments before. I pivoted with my hands on the front edge of his seat, scissored my legs and kicked one of the world's most beautiful women full in the face. In slow motion, I saw her nose fracture and the blood spray out.

She screamed, letting go of the machete. It bounced away under one of the neighbouring tables. Landing in a crouch, I grabbed the legs of Asher's chair and wrenched it out from under him. Then I swung it through a hundred and eighty degrees like a hammer thrower going for Olympic gold. It connected with the side of Marilyn Monroe's head and she crashed off the side of the table, taking the beaded lamp with her, and showed the room exactly what she was wearing under that famous white dress.

The place was in uproar by then. Dorothy Parker had leaped to her feet while Groucho Marx dived under the table. Oscar Wilde was fumbling inside his tailcoat.

Some premonition just gave me the time to mutter, "Oh shit..." from between clenched teeth before he pulled out an Uzi machine pistol on a shoulder-strap and grabbed at the trigger.

Dorothy Parker went down flailing in the first burst. I dived on top of Asher, taking one round in the left arm and a second just above my left hip in the process. Both stung like a bastard.

Cursing, I rolled with him under the overhanging cloth of the next table, discovering—painfully—where Marilyn Monroe's discarded machete had come to rest. I hefted it in my right hand, which was the only one still functioning. Above us, the panic was full scream ahead, accompanied by the sounds of a mortally wounded piano and a symphony of breaking glass.

Asher saw the blood and paled. "Charlie—!"

I growled, "Stay down," gripped the machete and low-crawled out into a lethal forest of running feet.

A woman's stiletto heel stamped into the back of my right hand, momentarily skewering it to the floor. I let out an unheard roar of pain. Oscar Wilde was still spraying the room with 9mm rounds at a rate of nine-hundred-and-fifty a minute. Somewhere under that coat, he must have had a stack of spare magazines.

I flexed my injured hand. I could still just about make a fist, but trying to wield the machete with any force or accuracy was a non-starter. Instead, I reared up from behind the table and flung it awkwardly at the gunman like a boomerang I prayed wasn't going to come back.

At the last moment, Oscar Wilde caught sight of the weapon flashing towards him.

He ducked and spun.

It was the wrong move.

The blade was honed like a razor. It sliced straight through the carotid artery at the side of his exposed neck. He lost his grasp of the Uzi and dropped to his knees, already starting to fade.

"Alas," he muttered, "I am dying beyond my means…"

Staying low—OK, sagging—I checked the room. As far as I could tell everybody was running away rather than charging towards us.

"OK, Asher," I called. "Show's over."

No response.

Oh shit…

Clumsily, I dropped to one knee and lifted the edge of the tablecloth. All I could see of Asher was a pair of black-clad legs ending in leather-soled shoes without a hint of wear. I jerked the tablecloth off completely and saw the rest of him on the far side. He had ignored my warning and followed me out into the line of fire. Blood oozed from the bullet holes in his jacket. Those blue eyes stared right through me.

I slumped to the floor and found myself at eye level with Groucho Marx who was lying under the next table, still clutching his cigar.

"Well, I've had a perfectly wonderful evening," he said. "But this wasn't it."

———

I SURFACED through a glutinous morass with a tube down my throat, fighting the overwhelming urge to vomit.

"Take it easy, Charlie," said a calm voice somewhere above me. "Just gotta unhook the main sensor umbilical… OK, you're all clear. Welcome back."

I sat up, dripping the pale green slime that was, so I'd been told, some kind of conductive fluid 'to enhance the full-body experience'. I ripped the tube out of my mouth with a hiccupping heave like a cat bringing up a fur-ball.

As I did so I realised I'd used both hands. I spread them out in front of me. No holes, no blood, and only a distant twinge.

The technician, Sherwin, grinned at me expectantly.

"So, what did you make of your first virtual reality trip? Pretty awesome, huh?"

I rubbed reflectively at my hip. "Are things *supposed* to hurt that much?"

"Ah, the boss had me ramp up the pain replication inputs so if you take a hit you can *really* imagine what the real thing feels like."

"It would have been nice if he'd mentioned that going in." I half-climbed, half-slithered out of the immersion tank. "Because some of us don't need to use our imagination, thanks."

He paled a little and suddenly found the need to give his full attention to wiping the gunk off the sensors and coiling them into a sterilisation tray. For a few moments, the only sound was the immersion tank draining like the last of the bathwater disappearing down the plughole.

We were in a small room with soundproofing material covering the walls. Apart from the tank, the overhead umbilical feed, and a steel trolley like you'd find in an operating theatre, it was empty of other equipment. I supposed that having spent a good chunk of his considerable fortune developing this VR technology, Asher wanted the brains of it kept well away from prying eyes or fingers.

"Speaking of the boss," I said at last, "where is he?"

"Oh, um, I guess his nurse has taken him back to his quarters. He'll be OK in a half-hour or so," Sherwin said cheerfully. "It always takes him a little while to get over being dead."

———

SHOWERED, dressed and feeling almost in touch with reality again, I found Brant, Asher's head of security, waiting for me in what I'd heard referred to as the den. It was more like the library of a very upmarket gentleman's club, complete with a mahogany-beamed ceiling, clusters of wingback chairs, and flock wallpaper so deep you could wade in it. All that was needed to complete the picture was for some elderly colonel to quietly snuff it behind his copy of the *Financial Times*.

Brant did not seem entirely at home in such surroundings. He was an ex-Navy SEAL—a fact you could tell just by looking— but it was not his job to blend. Brant organised the highly visible security around the mansion on the edge of Falls Lake, just north of Raleigh in North Carolina, and the ten acres of grounds and gardens that went with it.

From what I'd seen on the way in, he was doing a damn good job. The surveillance gear was high grade and well positioned. His team of former military or law enforcement personnel knew what was expected and could be relied upon to think on their feet.

And beneath the more noticeable patrols of men with guns and dogs were layers of covert electronic security that meant a mouse would have a hard time sneaking through. The only extra I could think of was real-time satellite tasking, and I wouldn't put it past Brant to call in a few favours if he felt the need.

All this to protect a man who hadn't set foot outside the property for sixteen years.

As I strolled towards Brant, I reminded myself not to limp from the phantom gunshot wounds. Wasn't *so* long ago I was trying not to limp from the real ones.

"Handled yourself OK in there," Brant said by way of greeting, and although he didn't add the words 'for a woman' I heard them all the same. "Not your fault the boss can't take orders."

"Is today typical of the kind of thing that's been happening?"

He nodded. "Just about every visit to La-La-Land over the past month, he comes out in a virtual body bag."

"Has the system been hacked?"

"Sherwin's the guy you'd have to ask about that. He starts talking schematics and I understand maybe one word in ten." He ran a frustrated hand over his close-cropped hair. "What I *do* know is, the whole system's standalone, completely unplugged from the 'Net. Only way anyone could insert a virus would be from *inside* the perimeter."

"Getting in is as close to impossible as makes no difference," I agreed—flattering, but true. "You've got this place sewn up tighter than a fish's armpit."

He showed his teeth briefly in satisfaction. "Watertight."

"So, what do you think is going on here?"

"It would be speculation on my part, but I'd guess somebody knows they can't get to him out there in the real world, so they're trying to take away the only thing he's got left."

———

A LOW HUM preceded Asher's arrival, his electric wheelchair moving fast enough across the tiled floor that the uniformed nurse at his shoulder had to move briskly to keep pace.

"Hey Charlie," he rasped, "how're you feeling?"

The irony of having my 'dead' principal inquire after the health of his bodyguard was not lost on me.

Asher Campbell Cooper III was still a force of nature regardless of the circumstances of the meeting. According to the background dossier I'd read before heading down from New York, back when Asher was nineteen he'd inherited a modest amount from his father. He used the money to launch himself into the rapidly expanding world of the Internet in the early 'nineties and within ten years was running one of the largest service providers of wireless, satellite and cable on the Eastern seaboard.

From the file, the appearance he'd chosen for his VR avatar was based pretty much on the way he'd actually looked in younger days. Something of a playboy, he'd married a beauty queen and taken up motorsport. Had his cake, eaten it, licked up the crumbs and gone back for more.

The pessimists would have said it couldn't last.

It didn't.

A high-speed freak racing accident, a structural failure, a high-temperature engine fire and a methanol explosion. They all combined to produce the man in the wheelchair with an irreparably damaged spinal cord and third-degree burns that covered more than half his body. He'd lost the fingers of his right hand as well as his right eye and ear. Because he no longer had a recognisable nose, a permanent oxygen supply had been tubed into his chest to boost his seared lungs. Despite enduring years of surgical procedures, his face still had the appearance of an ice sculpture left out in the sun.

Yeah, the irony of *him* enquiring after *my* health was definitely not lost on me.

"I'm fine," I said now. "A great improvement on the last time I was shot—or stabbed for that matter."

He laughed. It sounded like a handful of grit thrown into a blender.

"Not many people get their head around it so fast. Nice job."

"It would have been better if I'd kept you alive in there," I said. "At least to the end of the first day."

"Well, at least you got to experience the craziness first-hand."

"Before we went in, you said it would be 'dinner with some old friends'," I said. "I assume the cabaret wasn't part of the plan?"

"Marilyn Monroe going postal on my ass? No, ma'am."

I paused. "How far do you trust your tech guy, Sherwin?"

"All the way," he said without hesitation. He swivelled the eye that worked in Brant's direction.

"Sherwin passes all the regular polygraph tests," Brant said. "His financials are clean and there are no threats to his family."

"Who else has the expertise to engineer that kind of scenario?"

"Maybe a handful of people in the world. But you forget—I use the technology for my own…diversion. I'm nobody's competition. They gain nothing by sabotaging my system."

"So, who *might* gain something?"

Asher's shoulder gave a convulsive twitch that might once have been a shrug. "I have no idea."

"What about the staff? Friends, family, business associates?"

"Brant vets everyone who works for me."

I didn't ask who vetted Brant—probably the CIA.

"Plus everyone who enters the house undergoes a covert scan for weapons, bugs or other electronic devices," Brant put in.

I didn't rise to that one. "You hired me for personal protection and that means cure as much as prevention. I'm going to need to talk to everyone, including your family."

"Yeah, well. Good luck with that."

———

HAVING STRUCK out with the staff—as I'd known I would but still had to go through the motions—I moved on to the family. And working on the theory that sibling rivalry can be the most vicious kind I started with Asher's younger brother, Michael.

On the surface, he seemed a viable suspect. Ten years Asher's junior, not as good looking, not as much of a go-getter. Michael was a solid kind of guy who would have been the pride of his parents...had his parents not also had a son like Asher to invite unfair comparison.

But after the accident, Michael got promoted to the number-one spot. He was now in command of the Internet giant his brother had started. The reports showed he had the smarts to know his limitations and surround himself with the right people. The business was sound, showing steady growth and the ability to innovate without overreaching itself.

Asher made the introductory call, and Michael's PA squeezed me in between meetings at their offices in downtown Raleigh.

"I'm sure you're anxious to get to the bottom of this," I said carefully as we shook hands. "Thanks for seeing me at such short notice."

"Well, Ash still has some pull around here," Michael said.

Rather than returning to his desk, he guided me to a cluster of low sofas overlooking the skyline. The building was impressive without being flashy, set in the heart of the city amid wide tree-lined streets.

I sat and raised an eyebrow. "I thought he was out of the company?"

"Oh, he is, don't get me wrong. He's a majority shareholder but draws no salary and he doesn't interfere with the direction I want to take things. Even so, he was the boss for a long time." He gave a shrug. "Old habits."

"If anything should happen to your brother, who gets his shares?"

"The family." He flushed. "I get some, if that's what you're driving at. The rest is split between our sisters—one in West Virginia, the other in Paris, France. And Mother, of course."

"But you would have a controlling interest?"

It took him a moment to answer that. The flush regrouped around the collar of his shirt and put up a second wave.

"Look, I realise you have your job to do, but please be

assured I am *not* trying to kill my brother—in this world or any other."

Behind us, the office outer door opened and Michael's PA hovered expectantly in the gap. He nodded to her and rose, buttoning his jacket.

"Like I said, Ash doesn't interfere. I can't say that would be the case if my sisters took control of his shares." He shook my hand again, held on a moment longer. "I'll level with you, Miss Fox. I cannot imagine what it must be like for my brother to be the way he is, but I hope I'll be forgiven for praying the poor bastard lives to a grand old age."

―――

"I STAYED by his side and nursed him as far back as he was coming, then I left," said the former beauty queen. You could still see it in the arrangement of her features, the slant of her bones.

"Why no divorce?" I asked.

She smiled, causing a dimple to appear in her right cheek. "Partly to spite his mother," she admitted easily. "And partly because we're Catholics and, old-fashioned as it may seem in this day and age, we don't hold with divorce. Besides, there's no need. Ash and I already live our separate lives and he was more than generous."

She waved an elegant hand to indicate the corner penthouse condo in the PNC Plaza building—one of the tallest in Raleigh. It was airy and modern, with cherry-planked floors and high ceilings. Worth a fraction of the Falls Lake mansion, but well outside my price bracket.

"And if your husband should die?"

To her credit, a flicker passed across her features that I didn't think was faked and the smile turned wry.

"Then our arrangement ends and I get zip," she said. "Mommy dearest saw to that."

―――

"A MOST UNSUITABLE MATCH," Mrs Campbell Cooper sniffed, sitting rigidly upright in her chair. "I said she would never stay loyal to my son and I was not disappointed."

Looking at the old woman, her face deeply etched with decades' evidence of disapproval, I could believe it.

"Can you think of anyone who might wish to disrupt Asher's forays into virtual reality?"

She was too ladylike to snort, but it was a near thing. "Video games," she uttered with icy contempt. "All he has left is a first-class brain and he's rotting it playing *video games*. It's a shameful waste of his talents."

If I squinted hard I could just about see her point. Before this job, the only contact I'd had with computer simulations was tactical weapons training. But for someone with Asher's permanent injuries, I reckoned she could have shown a little more compassion. First-class brain or no.

"What would you rather have him do?" I asked. I did my best to keep my voice neutral, but she heard the implied censure even so.

"*Do*? What do you *mean* what would I have him do?" she demanded. "What is he fit for?" She refolded her hands in her lap, the upper gripping tight to the one beneath as if to prevent it yanking at her own hair.

"So why not let him spend his time however he chooses?"

"Do you honestly think *I* have any say in the matter?" she shot back. She paused, but I'd succeeded in poking her with a sharp enough stick to provoke an outburst. She rose, preparing to sweep out of the room in that wonderful state known as high dudgeon. At the last moment, she hesitated just long enough for me to see the genuine anguish through the cracks in her formidable facade.

"We called him Asher. It means fortunate, blessed, and for a long time it seemed he was," she said. "But there isn't a day goes by when I don't wonder if they were gravely mistaken to pull him from the wreckage of that crash."

"JUST ABOUT ANYONE could upload some kinda virus if they were told how to go about it," Sherwin said a shade defensively. "And hey, it was me took this whole thing—the glitches that kept occurring in the program—to Brant in the first place. You've met the guy. Why would I go poke an angry bear with a stick if I didn't have to?"

I hid a smile at the outrage in his voice. "How real a danger could Asher be in from these 'glitches'?"

He shrugged. "Kinda hard to say. I mean, if somebody really had it in for the boss surely they'd just find a way to override the safety protocols instead?"

"Which would do what, exactly?" I asked.

He cast me a slightly disbelieving look that I had to ask. "Well, when he gets shot, or run down by a train, or trampled by wildebeest, or pushed off a cliff—all of which have happened recently. There was this one time—"

"Focus, Sherwin!"

"Oh, um, yeah. Well, it would be theoretically possible to induce such physical shock to his system that it would send him into cardiac arrest."

"But that's not the way the system's been hacked?"

He shook his head. "It's just the scenarios that are totally messed up." He looked about to say more but flicked me an unhappy glance instead.

"This whole thing is totally messed up," I said, "so if you have anything you want to share, however bizarre, please go ahead."

"Well, it's almost like whoever's doing this is not trying to kill him," he said unhappily. "This is more like…torture."

————

"I THINK I have a handle on what's going on," I said. "We need to meet."

"You have? That's great," Asher said, the damage to his voice making him hard to read over the phone. "I have just the scenario. You're gonna love it."

"Real world, real time, Asher."

"My dollar, my call," he responded. "Besides, you're in North Carolina. You can't leave without seeing the best it has to offer."

I bit back a pithy retort. "Well, you're the boss."

"Yes, ma'am," he said. "Have Sherwin get you kitted out and I'll see you on the other side."

———

THE GRIT of sand against my teeth this time was driven by a biting northeasterly rather than a gentle Saharan wind. I stood alongside Asher on a vast open stretch of dunes with a grey Atlantic ahead and a grey sky above. Both of us wore overcoats, hats, and gloves.

"Any of this seem familiar?" Asher asked.

I glanced around. The land rose steadily behind us. The only buildings nearby were wooden shacks, their timbers bleached silver by the elements. What appeared to be a bed sheet flew from one of them like a huge flag.

Then, from the far side of the largest shack, a group of half a dozen men appeared, hauling a contraption that looked both heavy and flimsy at the same time. It was half hang-glider, half children's kite, held together with string and bicycle chains and mounted on a pair of wagon wheels.

"My God," I murmured. "The Wright brothers. We're at Kitty Hawk."

Asher nodded. "Kill Devil Hills on the Outer Banks, to be precise. Kitty Hawk is a couple of miles further up. It's December seventeenth, 1903 and we're about to witness the dawn of the aviation era."

I didn't point out that this was a mere virtual reconstruction, no more real than watching a play.

"You wanted to talk, so talk," Asher invited. "Don't worry, they won't do anything momentous until we're ready."

It was hard not to be fascinated as we strolled closer. The men wrestled the machine onto a narrow wooden rail in the sand and lifted the cartwheel bogeys out from under each wing.

"I talked to your family," I said. "Your mother has taken your condition hard."

I caught no glimpse of emotion on the smooth features of Asher's avatar. His eyes were on the two brothers, Wilbur and Orville, fussing around their craft. Wilbur was the taller of the two, clean-shaven and balding. They shared only a passing resemblance.

"Mother was always my greatest supporter and my sternest critic," Asher said at last. "I know how difficult it's been for her to see me as I am now—on the outside."

"She thinks you might have been better off if they'd left you in the burning wreck."

I watched his face as I spoke and saw he'd heard this all before—probably from the lady herself. She didn't strike me as the kind who'd keep a grievance silent.

He glanced down at me. I'd noticed before that he'd programmed himself with extra height. Either that or made the rest of us shorter.

"She's never had any trouble speaking her mind. Mostly, it's refreshing. Besides, you must have thought the same thing, the first time you laid eyes on me?"

"Your mother's a daunting woman," I said, side-stepping his question. "Maybe, subconsciously, you're trying to please her."

"By trying to kill myself?" He laughed, a far more melodious sound than in real life. "If I truly wanted to die in here, then I've sure had plenty of opportunities."

"But you were always a thrill seeker, weren't you Asher—a risk taker? Where did it get you?"

"It got me a business empire. If I hadn't taken risks the company would never have gotten off the ground." He nodded towards the Flyer as the Wright brothers swung the propellers and the engine spat and coughed and roared its way to life. "It's amazing *that* thing ever did."

I ignored his attempt to change the subject. "The company has continued to prosper with your brother in charge, and I've never met a man more conservative. Must be tough to watch, especially for someone who considered himself indispensable."

Asher said nothing.

"It would be enough to make anyone wonder what had it all

been for?" I went on, just loud enough to be heard over the
Flyer's raucous exhaust note.

"You think I *want* to keep dying in here?"

"I think the prospect of dying is, for you, the last great adven-
ture," I said. "I think it's all you have left to live for."

Orville Wright climbed through the tangle of bracing struts to
lie on the lower wing. He took the Flyer's control levers, revved
the engine and released the wire holding him onto the track. The
craft lumbered forwards and wobbled slowly into the air.

A cheer went up from the assembled ground crew. Asher and
I watched as the bi-plane gradually gained both altitude and
airspeed.

After a moment I nudged his arm. "If you *are* serious about
your health, we should move." And when he blinked at me,
frowning, I added, "How long was the first powered flight
supposed to last?"

"Around twelve seconds…"

Above us, the bi-plane went into a high banked turn and
swooped downwards with increasing agility.

"I get the feeling this has suddenly turned into the crop-
duster scene from *North By Northwest*," I said. "Move! *Now!*"

There wasn't a handy cornfield to hide in, but the wooden
hangar where the Flyer had been stored was standing open and
empty. I dragged Asher inside by the lapels of his overcoat and
almost flung him against the back wall.

The bi-plane buzzed the roof low enough to make the whole
building shudder and raced away to make another run.

"Are you hoping that if you die in here often enough, one
day it will really happen?"

"You're crazy," he said. "If I was trying to kill myself I could
have removed the safeties and been dead long before now."

"But where's the sporting uncertainty in that? Where's the
thrill?" I threw back. "And you're forgetting—a man who won't
go against the Church to divorce his wife certainly wouldn't
countenance the sin of suicide."

I'd nailed it. I could see it in his face. I let go of his coat and
stepped back.

"Take this as my resignation," I said. "Now get me out of this pantomime."

"Please, Charlie—"

I silenced him with a glare. "I can work with a client who doesn't want to die," I said. "But there's fuck all I can do with one who doesn't want to live."

———

More to Read!

If you liked this, then you may also like the later Charlie Fox novels, where she is in full-blown professional bodyguard mode. Why not take a look at CHARLIE FOX: BODYGUARD eBoxset of books 4, 5, and 6? And please check out the rest of the series **here**.

8

RISK ASSESSMENT

EVER SINCE I first discovered that not only were the Sherlock Holmes stories first published in serial form in the Strand Magazine *but that the magazine was still going—and still publishing crime fiction—it's been a small ambition of mine to have a story appear in those pages.*

Then, a couple of years ago, one of my American publishers snagged the attention of the Strand's *editor, Andrew Gulli. He agreed to consider a story from me, but the brief was so open I had instant brain fade over what* kind *of story I should write.*

Not long afterwards, I happened to be renewing my motor insurance over the phone. As I happily gave all my personal details to the (blameless, I'm sure!) guy at the other end of the line, it gradually dawned on me that, if anyone was nefariously inclined, this might be a perfect opportunity for a serial killer to select his victims…

The story appeared in Issue 51 of the Strand Magazine, *with illustrations by Jeffrey B McKeever, and very proud I am, too.*

———

IT'S her voice that lures him in. Kind of husky, as if she's smiling as she speaks. As if she's happy to be spending part of her Saturday morning on the phone, talking to someone like him.

She tells him her name is Helen. From her date of birth, he calculates she is thirty-two. Seven years his senior, but he doesn't care about a little thing like that. Her postcode puts her in the heart of the Derbyshire Peak District.

"Lovely area of the country," he says approvingly. "Except in the winter, I imagine."

"It can be a bit tricky when it snows," she agrees. "But I'm on the edge of a village, and they usually plough the road for the school bus."

"I expect that pleases everyone—except the kids."

She laughs. "Yes…I expect it does." Her tone suggests she's never given it much thought.

No kids, then.

She's divorced, she tells him, when he asks her marital status. There's a cheerful note to her voice. If it gave her a bad time, it is now put firmly behind her. Maybe she was the instigator?

Can't have come out of it too badly, though. The property has a name rather than a number. And when she gives him the registration, make and model of her car, it's a mid-range BMW coupé less than two years old. Not cheap, by any stretch. She's never had an accident, and her licence is clean.

"Do you have use of any other vehicles—belonging to another family member, perhaps, someone living at the same address?"

"There's nobody else here, only me. But I have a motorcycle. Does that count?"

"Of course it does." He's surprised, but not unpleasantly so. "So, you're a bit of a biker as well, are you?"

"Oh yes. Nothing quite like it in the summer, especially through the Peak District National Park—you know, over Cat and Fiddle, or across Saddleworth Moor. Wonderful twisty roads."

"Bit isolated, though. Aren't you worried about breaking down on your own in the middle of nowhere?"

"Not really. Modern British bikes are a lot more reliable than they used to be in the bad old days."

"You be careful of the speed traps, then, or that licence of yours won't stay clean much longer."

She laughs again. It plugs straight into his nervous system, zeros in on his groin. He shifts in his chair, uncomfortable, hurries on with his questions.

Both the car and motorcycle are kept in the garage overnight, which is integral to the house.

"And you always put the car away? Only, if you ever leave it out on the driveway, you're better off saying so, just in case."

"No, no," she says. "I have a remote for the up-and-over door, so when I get home from work I drive straight in."

"Very handy."

"It is! Especially if it's raining. Lazy, I know, but useful for unloading shopping or what-have-you into the utility room."

"Is the garage covered by an alarm of some sort?"

"I've never bothered. It's very quiet round here. I don't think there's been a burglary anywhere in the village for years."

"Well, that should help, anyway."

"Oh, good."

"Let me just have a little look and see what we can do for you…"

He finishes keying in her information, hits Return and waits until his screen refreshes with quotes from all the major insurance companies. For the cover she is after, the top quote is competitive. He scrolls down until he finds an alternative, one where the premium is almost double. He reads that out instead, his voice regretful.

"I'm afraid that's not as good as my current insurer," she tells him. "I've had the renewal through, but I always like to check I'm getting a good deal."

"Ah, what a shame. Well, that's the best price coming up on my system, I'm afraid. I hope you'll give us another chance when your bike insurance falls due. Now, is there anything else I can help you with today?"

After she disconnects he sits for a while, isolated in his cubicle with the hubbub of the office floor going on unheard around him. He is a submerged rock in a sea of choppy waters, unmoving and unmoveable.

He taps on his keyboard, calls up Helen's details again and takes another look. Remembering. Discreetly, he slides his smartphone from a pocket, photographs the information on the screen.

Then he follows protocol, hits the Delete key and watches as every last traceable byte of her disappears into the server's cyber shredder.

―――――

HE WAITS A MONTH. Long enough for her to have phoned another half-dozen companies and brokers, gone through the details over and over. Long enough for her to have arranged new car insurance elsewhere and forgotten all about the company he works for and his name, which he takes such care to mumble. For the mindless sub-routines of her daily life to go on, unsuspecting.

Long enough for him to research Helen on social media. She's been cagey with how much she gives out on Facebook and Instagram, but he has her full name, address and birthday. She's easy enough to identify.

He takes the time to study photographs of her in a bikini on the beach in Mauritius. Snapshots posted of a holiday with her sister. To locate her house on Google Earth, and do a virtual drive-by on Street View to check out the proximity of her neighbours. He even runs a search on local police response times, and is heartened by the lacklustre result. All done, of course, using the downloaded Tor browser designed to cloak the user's identity for his forays into the Dark Web.

Helen is petite and blonde and pretty. Different enough in type from his last…selection to confuse the profilers.

He takes the time to plan.

And his anticipation grows into hunger.

―――――

WHEN THE DAY arrives he is more than ready. He drives a nondescript Toyota borrowed from the office pool and signed for with an illegible squiggle. He has already lined the boot of the car with polythene sheeting, available from any builder's yard, double-layered. He has temporarily disabled the boot's internal release handle, too. Not that he expects she will be in any condition to operate it. But best to be sure.

He dresses in clothing bought from charity shops spread around the city, including shoes a size too large, that have a wear pattern not his own. If you're going to leave evidence, it may as well work for you as against you.

He will burn everything when he is done.

He drives the motorway miles sedately, baseball cap pulled down over his forehead, sunglasses covering his eyes. The registration number on the car *is* a match to a Toyota of the same model, year and colour—just not this one. The reg belongs to a vehicle currently in long-term parking at Heathrow while its elderly owners enjoy an anniversary cruise. He arranged their travel cover before the trip.

He has left his smartphone at home, where its GPS chip is dutifully recording its blameless position, should anyone ever feel the need to check.

He parks in a lay-by—another product of his Street View recces—and heads across the fields, following a footpath he located on a local ramblers' website. It is chilly enough for hat, gloves, and scarf not to raise suspicions. Openly, he carries a lead for a nonexistent dog to both justify his presence and make it seem more innocuous.

In his pocket is a knife, and a set of plastic zip-ties.

He picks out the rear aspect of her house through the trees, but keeps walking all the way to the road, then turns around and slowly retraces his steps. It is a quarter to five in the afternoon in early March. He waits until lights start to come on in the far village. No lights come on in Helen's house.

He makes his move.

The back door leading into the utility room behind the garage is UPVC with a double-glazed upper panel and a standard cheap euro cylinder lock. He bumps it in less than two minutes, using a custom key he made courtesy of a YouTube 'How To'.

And he's in.

For a moment he stands motionless on the doormat, listening to the sounds of an empty house. The cycle of the fridge compressor, the tick of a radiator valve in the hallway.

Nobody home.

He maps out in his mind the route she will take when she

gets back from her office job in Administration. From garage to utility room and through to the kitchen. The garage has the usual detritus. Gardening tools, a barbecue and a muddy bicycle. There is a car-sized void in the centre of the space, years of old oil-stains on the bare concrete floor.

The motorcycle she mentioned sits shrouded against the back wall. He's tempted to take a look, but can't risk her noticing any disturbance of the cover, bright in her headlights as she drives in.

He wonders who will own it next.

He shakes himself, checks the time, and closes the door between garage and utility on his way back into the house. Where to wait for her? Always the question. Deep enough inside that she won't baulk from entering. Not so deep that she has a chance to turn and run.

He decides on the kitchen itself. It is shaped so that he will be out of sight of the doorway, and Helen is tidy enough not to leave any possible weapons close to hand on the gleaming countertops.

A shiver of excitement passes through him. The waiting is exquisite torture.

He wishes it were over.

He wishes it would last forever.

————

LIGHTS SWING into the driveway at five-forty-three. He hears the whirr and clank of the electric garage door slowly rising. The car's engine sounds louder, more boomy, as she pulls inside. Then dies away to silence.

A car door opens and closes, the bleep of the alarm, together with the solid thunk of the door locks engaging. Footsteps, approaching…

He is holding his breath.

She enters the kitchen in a flurry of cold air, heads to the table to deposit her bag and the coat slung over her arm. He is close enough to smell her shampoo, her perfume. She turns away to reach for the kitchen light.

Now.

He steps up, steps in, grabbing her upper body from behind. The knife is out ready in his hand, the blade at her throat.

Mine!

It is the last thing he remembers.

———

AWARENESS RETURNS SLOWLY. And with it pain.

Pain in his limbs, his head, his gut. He is slumped in an upright chair with his chin propped on his chest. He doesn't know how long he's been there, but when he raises his head his neck clicks stiffly.

The room is stark and bright beyond his slitted eyelids. Cautiously, he rolls his shoulders, finds his hands secured behind him and feet bound at the ankles to the legs of the chair. He thrashes against the constriction on a surge of pure panic. Almost instantly he stills from the spike of pain as the bones grate in his right wrist and forearm. He fights back nausea.

Eyes wide now, he realises he is in the dining room. Blood from his nose, his mouth, has splashed onto the front of his shirt.

What the hell happened?

There is a blank space where the memory should be. It terrifies him.

So do the footsteps he hears in the hallway.

The woman who enters is a stranger. Medium height, medium build. Without the long blonde wig, her hair is a choppy bob in shades of red and gold. She is wearing jeans, boots and a leather jacket. Over her arm, on a hanger, is the business suit she wore in her guise as Helen.

But it is her hands that drag his focus.

She wears black latex gloves, and is carrying a knife.

His knife.

"Wh–who—?"

Carefully, she lays the suit across the dining table, moves to within a few feet of him and holds up the knife. Something about the practised way she does it sends another shiver through him. It is a long way from excitement this time.

"My name's Fox," she says then. "I'd offer to shake hands but —," a shrug, "—I see you're a little tied up at the moment."

The name means nothing to him. He is certain he's never had *her* details up on his computer screen. She sees his confusion, adds, "At this stage, Drew, all you really need to know is that *I* know exactly who *you* are. And what's more, I know exactly what you're about."

"Where is she?" He can't help blurting out the question. He feels cheated, betrayed.

"Helen? She isn't here," the woman says. "In fact, she was never *going* to be."

His mouth opens, gulps like a drowning fish.

"But—?"

The front door slams. The woman calling herself Fox steps sideways, calls over her shoulder, "In here."

Another woman comes in—taller, more elegant, long dark hair and long bones. Still not Helen. She pauses when she sees him, her expression one of guarded distaste. She also wears gloves, to hand over what looks like a set of keys…

"Did you find it?" Fox asks.

The other nods. "Just down the road. Fake plates," she says, which jolts him as much as the knife. She is pale in the artificial light as she adds, "The whole of the back is prepped for a body dump."

"Of course it is," Fox murmurs. She turns to him, inspecting the edge of the blade, the weight, and the balance. "So, now I've caught him for you, Madeleine, what do you want to do with him?"

"Hand him over to the police?" the dark haired woman offers, but there's a dubious note in her voice.

"If that's what you want, but you know as well as I do that you can't prove what he's done. As far as they're aware, it's a first offence. Given a half-decent brief, and a judge with a room-temperature IQ, he might even get away with it."

For the first time since he came round and found himself tied to a chair, he begins to hope that all is not quite lost.

"And you've broken my bloody arm, you bitch," he blurts, finding both voice and bravado. "I ought to sue."

"You put a knife to my throat." She pins him with a dead eye. "So, *I* ought to have ripped your arm off at the shoulder and beat you to death with the wet end. Sad, isn't it, how we can't always have what we want."

"So, what *are* we going to do with him?" the dark-haired woman, Madeleine, asks.

"How many has he taken, do you think?"

A frown. "Four in the last year—that we know of, anyway. Could be more if he has some secondary method of selection."

He goes hot and then cold as his body primes for flight. There's a hollow feeling beneath his ribs. "You can't prove anything…"

"Prove? Maybe not." Fox moves in front of him, forcing his neck to crane as he looks up into her face. "But *know,* that's something else again. Because my friend here is an expert with computers. And *you* are not."

She leans a little closer. He tries not to cringe back but he's afraid now. Seriously afraid. Of what he sees in her eyes. And of what is missing. He sees that same look—that same lack—when he stands in front of the bathroom mirror every morning. He recognises it in others.

There seems no point in further denial. He asks, almost in a whisper, "How did you know?"

She glances across at her companion, a 'do you want to tell him or shall I' kind of a look. Madeleine shrugs.

"When you're at work, your phone connects to the company Wi-Fi network. Any photos you take during working hours, it automatically backs up to the cloud. And when I was brought in to run a cyber-security audit. I found those pictures."

He lets his eyes close briefly, rallies his bravado for a last stand. "Fuck you. You've got nothing." He hates how desperate he sounds, even so.

"It would be difficult, but not impossible," Fox allows. "Prosecutors don't like to chance having the 'victim' resurface after a guilty verdict's been handed down. Still, there *have* been murder convictions in the past without a body."

He says nothing, swallows and knows she registers his fear.

"But somehow I don't think any of *your* victims are going to reappear, are they?"

"What victims? *You* attacked *me* here. It's your word against mine."

"He has a point, Charlie," Madeleine says. "I just hate to think, after everything…there's a chance he might walk."

Her voice holds indecision he doesn't immediately understand. And when he does, the fear starts to tingle across his shins again, to roil in his gut.

Charlie Fox simply regards him, flatly. The knife is still held lightly between her gloved fingers.

"He might," she agrees. "Except…"

His eyes swivel from one to the other and back again. He wants to wait her out, but can't stand the tension. "Except *what*?" he demands.

"Look around you, Drew. You're the one tied to a chair. I'm the one with the knife. You've already lined the back of your car with plastic. You even brought your own shovel." She smiles. It is not reassuring. "Do you really think I'd let all that effort go to waste…?"

———

More to Read!

If you liked this, then you may also like the later Charlie Fox novels, where she is in full-blown professional bodyguard mode. Why not take a look at CHARLIE FOX: BODYGUARD eBoxset of books 4, 5, and 6? And please check out the rest of the series **here**, including BAD TURN, which sees Charlie again faced with doing the wrong things for the right reasons.

9

HOUNDED

I grew up reading the Sherlock Holmes stories of Sir Arthur Conan Doyle, so it was a real treat for me to be approached by the editors of the For The Sake Of The Game anthology, to write a story inspired by the Conan Doyle canon.

The contributors were told they could approach this from any direction, from inserting Holmes into an alternative setting, reworking an existing story with a new slant, or simply writing something 'in the style of'. I chose to attempt my own version of one of my favourite tales, Hound Of The Baskervilles. It was probably the closest Conan Doyle came to casting his characters into the world of close protection, which is the particular expertise of my main protagonist, Charlie Fox, so I knew she could have a major part to play.

And when I re-read the original, I realised the sub-plot was just perfect as the main strand of the story for Charlie. So, I brought that to the fore, and left all the business with the 'hell hound' to Holmes and Watson, which is only as it should be.

———

"Excuse me, gentlemen, is anyone sitting here?"

The men looked up from their table with the resigned irritation of travellers who thought they'd managed to get three seats together in a First Class compartment, without having to endure the company of a stranger.

One of them—youngish and tall, with a nose he could have used to spear pickles out of a jar—peered rather pointedly over his gold-framed spectacles at the adjacent table across the aisle. It had only a middle-aged, middle-class couple in occupation, although they'd sprawled their iPads and iPhones and papers across the surface to stake their claim.

I followed his gaze and produced a rueful smile.

"I don't go by train very often," I confided as I slid into the remaining seat. "But when I do I'm afraid I really can't face backwards. Gives me motion sickness."

"Ah," said the man. "Have you thought of taking hyoscine hydrobromide of some kind? It's available at any pharmacy without a prescription."

Before I could answer that, one of the others—an older man with a bushy moustache and the upright spine of the ex-soldier —cut in with, "Or antihistamines? A little less effective, perhaps, but fewer side-effects. Hyoscine may make you drowsy, my dear."

Instinctively, I glanced at the third man. He was small and sturdy, his hands and face tanned as much by wind as by sun. He grinned at me from under thick black eyebrows.

"Hey, no use looking to me for advice. These two guys are the physicians. The ginger tea my mom used to make whenever *I* got sick, that's about all I could suggest."

My first thought was *American*, but the slightly Scottish inflection on the word "about" tipped him farther north.

"Is that a Canadian accent I hear?"

The bushy eyebrows wriggled like two hairy caterpillars on his forehead, and his grin, if anything, widened.

"Good call," he said. "Most folks over here mistake me for a Yank."

"Ah, well, I shouldn't let it worry you." I returned his smile. "*Some* folk over here mistake *me* for a lady."

He laughed out loud at that, and after a moment the two doctors allowed themselves a small twist of the lips that might have passed for amusement. The Canadian, meanwhile, leaned across the table with a weathered hand outstretched. "Henry Baskerville."

I took his hand, not without caution, and received a robust shake that threatened to bounce my shoulder out of its socket. Still, at least there were two professionals nearby who could have put it back for me.

"Charlie Fox," I said. "Nice to meet you, Henry."

The beaky-nosed doctor cleared his throat, murmured, "It's *Sir* Henry, actually."

"Really? Should I curtsey?"

"Oh, not on my account, I assure you. A few months ago I was farming in Alberta province. Then my uncle, Sir Charles Baskerville, died suddenly, and now I find myself a baronet with a country estate in Devonshire."

"I thought your last name rang a bell. There was something unusual about your uncle's death, wasn't there? Enough to make the national news, anyway."

"Ah, you're referring to the pet story of my family—the hell hound." Sir Henry smiled again at his own pun. "I've heard of it ever since I was in the nursery, but I never thought of taking it seriously until now."

The doctors' eyes flicked towards each other. Only a tiny movement, but I caught it nonetheless.

"Sir Charles died of dyspnoea—difficulty breathing—and cardiac failure," the beaky-nosed doctor said. "The post-mortem examination showed long-standing organic heart disease. Indeed, as his medical practitioner I had urged him to seek specialist advice about his health. But…" He gave a shrug.

"I'm sure you did everything you could for your patient," I offered. "Urging him is one thing, but I don't suppose you could exactly truss him up like a Sunday roast and deliver him to Harley Street, could you?"

He unbent enough then to introduce himself as Dr James Mortimer. That left the older of the men, who quickly followed suit, even though recognising him was the reason I'd begged the spare seat at their table in the first place.

"Dr John Watson."

I manufactured a reasonable facsimile of surprise. "Of

course," I said. "I follow your blog. The exploits of Sherlock Holmes, consulting detective. If even half of it is true, it makes fascinating reading."

"If anything, I tend to play *down* some of the more sensational aspects of Holmes's cases," Watson said, looking almost sheepish.

A firm nudge against my leg beneath the table had me looking down, to find a curly-haired spaniel eyeing me dolefully. I stroked the dog's ears, and said, "Do I take it there might be a hint of the sensational going on in Devon?"

"Indeed not," Watson denied quickly. "Or Sherlock Holmes himself would be travelling with us."

"Which, plainly, he is not," Mortimer added, trying for an air of nonchalance that he failed to pull off.

"Even so, to bring along not one but *two* doctors, Sir Henry, you must be wary of something serious happening to you?"

"I guess it might look that way," said the baronet. "And there have been a couple of interesting occurrences since I got to England. I don't mind admitting I feel safer in company."

Aware of a certain relief, I opened my mouth to ask more about that, but Watson jumped into the gap with a question about my own reason for heading down to Dartmoor.

My turn to shrug. "Oh, I've booked a week away in one of those little holiday cottages on the moor," I said, still fussing the spaniel under the table as an excuse not to make eye contact. "It's more a yurt than a cottage, from the pictures I've seen. A bit basic, but the season's just about over, so I'm told I'll have the whole development to myself."

"I know the ones. They *are* rather remote," Mortimer said. "Are you sure you'll be all right out there on your own?"

"I needed a get-away-from-it-all break." The story tripped convincingly from my tongue. "Having no internet and no cellphone coverage sounded like a blessing rather than a curse."

I didn't think it necessary to mention the military-grade GPS unit tucked into my rucksack. Nor the 9mm SIG Sauer lying snug in a concealed-carry rig at the small of my back.

If they weren't here to interfere in my business, at this stage of the operation I had no intention of interfering in theirs.

———

THE STATION WAS TINY, little more than a roadside halt, bordered by a white fence from which hung flower boxes overflowing with late blooms. Sir Henry, the two doctors and I were the only passengers to climb down when the train made its brief stop.

Two vehicles waited outside the gate, but neither of them was for me—or at least I hoped not, because as well as a Land Rover Discovery there was also a liveried police BMW with two officers in tactical black standing by. They eyed us with suspicion as we passed.

The Discovery driver hopped out and opened the rear doors to take his party and their bags. Mortimer lifted the wriggling spaniel into the rear luggage compartment.

I hovered, looking up and down the deserted road and frowning, until Sir Henry, who'd taken the front passenger seat, called to me through the open window.

"Hey, Miss Fox, you need a ride?"

"Well, it looks like mine hasn't turned up, for some reason. That's very kind. Are you sure I won't be taking you out of your way?"

"Dr Mortimer tells me we'll pass the cottages on our way to Baskerville Hall."

"In that case, I'd be very grateful to accept. I know I was hoping to do some walking while I'm here, but there *are* limits."

As the smallest, I squeezed into the middle of the rear seat, between the two doctors. The driver placed my rucksack in with the luggage and the spaniel. The dog huffed down the back of my neck through the grille that separated us.

As we set off, I asked, "Why the police presence?" with as much innocence as I could muster.

The driver spoke over his shoulder. "There's a prisoner escaped from HMP Dartmoor. He's been out three days now and they watch every road and station, but they've had no sight of him yet. The farmers here about don't like it, miss, and that's a fact."

"After three days in the outdoors without anything by way of food or shelter," I said, "he's unlikely to be much of a threat to anyone."

"Ah," the man said, "but it isn't like any ordinary convict. This is a man that would stick at nothing."

"Oh?" said Mortimer. "Who is he, Perkins?"

"It is Selden, the Notting Hill murderer."

I'd spent a lot of time over the last few years living and working outside the UK, but the man's crimes had been vicious enough to attract international coverage.

"And it will be dark by the time you reach your cottage tonight," Mortimer put in with a dubious glance. "Perhaps you should delay until daylight tomorrow?"

I made a show of indecision. "Well, if I might borrow a phone so I can call the woman who was supposed to meet me with the keys, I should be fine."

Perkins unhooked his elderly cellphone from its holder on the dashboard and passed it to me without hesitation. I dug the booking confirmation out of my pocket and dialled the number. A minute or so later I handed the phone back.

"It seems she mistook the time of my train and is shopping over in Exeter," I said. "She'll be on her way home shortly. If you'd drop me off by the cottage, I'm happy to wait there."

"Out of doors, with a man like Selden on the loose?" Sir Henry said. "I won't hear of it. Besides, the light will soon be gone, and the last thing Mr Holmes said to me when we left London was to quote one of the phrases from that queer old family legend: 'Avoid the moor in those hours of darkness when the powers of evil are exalted.' Come dine with us at the Hall and have this woman meet you there. I couldn't live with myself if you fell victim either to this psychopath or the infamous hound!"

———

WE SAW the twin crenellated towers of Baskerville Hall long before we reached the intricate wrought-iron gates. The original gate lodge was derelict, but a new construction had been started on the other side of the drive. Sir Charles Baskerville, I recalled, had made a fortune in South Africa. Clearly, he'd been spending lavishly on his property at the point of his demise.

An avenue of trees lined the driveway, darker in the falling light. The Discovery's headlights threw elongated shadows into the tunnel of thick foliage, creating an even more eerie effect.

"Was it here?" Sir Henry asked in a low voice. "That my uncle …?"

"No, no," Mortimer said. "In the Yew Alley, on the other side."

The avenue opened out onto a lawn area with the house centre stage. The central section was swathed in creepers, cut away from the odd window or coat of arms. The towers we'd seen protruded from the top, and a porch jutted out at the front. The wings at either side had to be later additions, in dark granite with mullioned windows. A few dingy lights showed through the glass, but overall it looked like someone had gone mad with low-energy bulbs and really needed to swap them out for much brighter LEDs.

We were met by the Barrymores, husband and wife, who had apparently looked after the Baskervilles for years. They didn't bat an eye at my unexpected inclusion for dinner. Still, they didn't have extra to cater for. Dr Mortimer made his excuses and disappeared with Perkins in the Discovery. Once I got inside, I discovered why he'd been keen to get home.

The interior of the Hall was as gloomy as it appeared from the exterior. The walls were hung with murky portraits of Baskervilles through the ages, painted by artists who'd evidently got bulk discount on tubes of Burnt Umber and Lamp Black.

The dining room, which opened out of the hallway, was even more depressing. It didn't help that both Sir Henry and Watson had worn dark suits for the journey. I had on a navy blue fleece and felt positively gaudy by comparison.

After we'd eaten—a subdued meal with little conversation—we moved through to another dimly lit room, this time containing glass-fronted bookcases and a full-size billiard table. The wind had begun to pick up across the moor, rattling the windows as if seeking an unguarded place to enter.

"My word, it isn't a very cheerful place," Sir Henry said. "I don't wonder that my uncle got a little jumpy, if he lived all alone in a house such as this."

The sweep of headlights across the front of the house and the crunch of tyres on the gravel heralded the arrival of the caretaker of the holiday cottages. She was a large lady who bustled in with great energy, in a long skirt and unbelted raincoat, so she took on the appearance of a galleon under sail.

I said my thanks to the household before being whisked away to bump across a moorland track in her elderly Daihatsu 4x4. She was full of apologies and explanations, and never seemed to stop talking long enough to draw breath.

The cottage was one of a group that had once been peasants' huts, huddled in a hollow on the moor to escape the worst of the winter gales. The sparse nearby trees all grew at extreme angles to show the direction of the prevailing wind. I reckoned that if I lived out here I'd soon develop a permanent lean from the force of it.

"I confess I half expected you to cancel, lovey, what with this madman loose on the moor. Shocking, isn't it? In fact, I'm in two minds about whether you *should* stay out here all alone, I really am."

The last thing I wanted was for her to try to stop me from staying. The cottage was isolated and unobserved—the perfect vantage point from which to study the habits of my target, and to finalise my plans.

"If they've had no sign of him in three days, he's probably long gone by now," I said quickly. "I'm sure I'll be fine."

Although the accommodation was tiny it was enough for my needs. Heating and cooking were via the wood-burning stove in one corner, but the building had been well insulated, and I'd been fed already, so I didn't feel the need to light the stove tonight.

Instead, I switched out the lamp and sat below the window, looking up at the clouds rushing past the stars in the light from a pale half moon, while I stripped, cleaned, and reassembled the 9mm pistol by touch alone.

———

THE FOLLOWING MORNING I woke early, splashed cold water onto my face, and shrugged into my clothes knowing I had a lot of ground to cover and limited time in which to cover it.

The wind of last night had died down. As I stepped outside I was immediately aware of a faint odour of wood smoke. I stilled in the watery sunshine and heard a shrill, burbling whistle that sounded very like an old-fashioned kettle coming to the boil.

Reaching behind me, I eased the semiautomatic pistol in its rig to make sure it wouldn't foul on my clothing, and moved softly towards the source of the sound.

Unless I was mistaken, it came from the end cottage of the little group. As I approached, I saw the door was slightly ajar, leaving a strip of internal frame visible along the leading edge.

I paused a second just outside, mind flashing through my options. Not the entry—that I could do in my sleep—but the excuse I'd need for it if the occupant turned out to be a legitimate guest.

"Don't stand on ceremony," called a man's voice from within. "I've taken the liberty of preparing breakfast for both of us."

He sounded friendly enough, but I've come across too many smiling killers not to draw the SIG first. Holding it down by my leg, I shoved the door open and slid rapidly to the side of the aperture as I went through.

A spare man with a thin face and high forehead sat with a chair pulled up close to the wood-burning stove, on the top of which he was nudging with a spatula at bacon, eggs, and tomatoes frying in a small pan. He barely glanced at me as I came in, but I got the impression there was little he didn't see.

"Ah, a woman of caution as well as action," he said. "Good. That makes things so much less worrisome."

It was not the opening gambit I'd expected, causing me to ask blankly, "How so?"

"Because clearly I need not concern myself with your safety while this man Selden is still at large, and therefore you will not distract me from the task at hand," he said as if it were obvious. He lifted the pan off the heat. "Now, there's bread on the table, if you wouldn't mind cutting a couple of slices? The kettle, as you no doubt heard, has just boiled. I can offer you Earl Grey or coffee—both black. No milk, I'm afraid."

"Excuse *me*, but my mother always warned me never to put anything offered by a stranger into my mouth."

He gave a bark of laughter, swapped the frying pan to his left hand and stuck out his right. "Your mother is evidently a woman of good sense and sound judgement," he said. "Sherlock Holmes, at your service."

I put away the SIG and shook his hand, murmuring a cautious, "I'm Charlie" as I did so.

"Well, Charlie, my thanks to you. It's due entirely to your arrival last night that I can indulge in a hot meal this morning."

"Ah, you mean if anyone saw the smoke"—I nodded to the wood-burner—"they would assume it was mine."

"Absolutely. So it's only right that I should offer to share my good fortune."

I hesitated a moment longer, then shrugged and moved across to the table. By the time I'd sliced two chunks from the crusty loaf, he'd served the contents of the pan and laid out cutlery. Automatically, I took the chair opposite the window and we both dug in. It felt somewhat bizarre to sit down to a camp-fire breakfast with such a man, only seconds after we'd met.

He ate with the same single-minded focus I imagined he did everything. Only when he'd finished the last bite, wiped his plate clean with bread, and sat back with his mug of tea, did he turn his scrutiny in my direction.

"Tell me, Charlie, how long is it since you were in the military?"

I allowed myself a raised eyebrow. "Not everyone who knows how to handle a firearm is necessarily an ex-squaddie."

"True. But in this country, where guns are far more uncommon than in America, it's certainly indicative. As is the way you lace your boots."

"Damn." I glanced down at my hiking boots, frowning. "Old habits, I suppose."

"Indeed."

"I take it that Dr Watson and Sir Henry are not aware of your presence?"

"Just so," Holmes agreed. "And I would be grateful if I could prevail upon you to keep them in ignorance of the fact. Our opponents in this case are formidable, and I thought it prudent to remain an unknown factor in the business, ready to throw in all of my weight at a critical moment."

"They won't hear anything from me," I said. "But I don't suppose you'd care to tell me what the '*business*' you're concerned with might be?"

He shook his head, smiling. "No more, I suspect, than you yourself would be willing to tell me what brings *you* to the wilds of Dartmoor."

I took a sip of my coffee, which was thick, dark and sweet, like treacle. "I *might* be here on a straightforward walking holiday …"

"But then again, you *might* not …"

"Care to hazard a guess?"

He looked offended. "I never guess. It is a shocking habit—destructive to the logical faculty."

"My apologies. To *deduce*, then?"

He put down his mug and leaned both elbows on the table top, steepling his fingers as he regarded me. I sat without fidgeting and stared right back.

"Hm. Whatever you did in the army, it was a role that was out of the ordinary," he said at last. "And your experiences either during your period of service or since have had a profound effect on you."

That was closer to the mark than I was expecting, even from a man with Holmes's reputation. I resisted the urge to shift in my seat and said only a noncommittal "Oh?"

"You are too intelligent, articulate, and far too aware of your surroundings to have been merely a 'squaddie', as you put it," he said. "By choosing a seat with your back to the wall, facing both doorway and window, you take great pains not to put yourself at a tactical disadvantage, despite the fact this puts me between you and any means of egress."

"From what I've read about you in Dr Watson's blog, you're pretty handy at Bartitsu. If anyone comes through that door, they'll have to deal with you first."

He ignored my flip remark, gesturing instead to the mug I was clutching. "You are clearly right handed, and yet—even after you have ascertained that I am not a threat—you are careful to drink only with your left, leaving your strong hand unencumbered."

"Perhaps it isn't *you* I'm worried about."

"Thus confirming that you have come to the moors with a purpose. One that is not without considerable dangers attached."

Still, I hedged. "Aren't you forgetting this prisoner on the run, Selden? My precautions could be all because of him."

"If you were so concerned about an escaped lunatic, you would not have come at all," Holmes said. "And he's still hereabouts, by the way, so do watch yourself."

"Thanks for the warning—and for breakfast," I said, rising. "I'll leave you to whatever it is you're working on." I stepped past him, pausing at the doorway. "Unless, of course, there's anything *else* about me you'd care to add?"

"You present quite the conundrum, Charlie. You have the appearance of someone who is only too willing to resort to violence, and yet is equally determined to avoid doing so, from which I might conclude that your own reasons for being here contain that combination." Holmes regarded me steadily, his smile no longer in evidence. "Be aware that I am dealing with an ugly, dangerous business, and if by any chance our undertakings should coincide, you will need all your skills about you."

———

I WALKED over rutted stone tracks into the nearest village of Grimpen. It was a low-lying place of cottages huddled down against the elements, with few people in sight. The only large buildings turned out to be the local pub and the house of Dr Mortimer. As I passed, I was amused to notice an old phrenology bust in the window of his surgery.

There was an open-all-hours village store, combining Post Office and greengrocer as well as a couple of café tables. They had Wi-Fi, though, and I was able to pick up my emails, including an attached folder of jpeg images that provided me with added motivation, if that were needed, to complete my task. I sent a brief response saying I was in position and had begun to recce for my opportunity to act.

I bought a few supplies, stowed them in my rucksack, and set off walking back. The day was clear, and the sun had solidified the turning colours of the moorland into shades of russet and gold. All-in-all, a lot cheerier looking than it had appeared last night.

According to my GPS unit it was about a 5.4km hike, and although the rough ground meant I had to take care where I put my feet, it was easy enough to give me thinking time. I would guess I was about halfway back to the cottage when someone shouted my name.

I turned quickly, to see two men approaching. One of them I knew already—Dr John Watson. The other I recognised, although we had not yet met, and for a moment I wished heartily that I had been either quicker or slower along the track.

"This is Jack Stapleton," Watson said when they'd caught up to me. "He lives at Merripit House. You may have seen it—or at least the smoke from the chimney—if you've had a chance to do any walking yet."

"Only into the village," I said, shaking Stapleton's hand. He had an expensive looking Nikon camera on a strap over his shoulder. I tried not to let the possible range of the telephoto lens bother me. "That's a serious piece of kit."

"I'm a naturalist," the man said. He was a little shorter than the doctor, clean-shaven, with fair hair showing beneath a battered straw hat. He lifted a shoulder to indicate the Nikon. "We don't catch butterflies in a net and pin them to a board anymore."

"I'm glad to hear it," I said, but photos of a different kind were printed large in my mind's eye. Photos of bruised and swollen flesh, and of long-term misery. I couldn't quite prevent myself adding in an entirely neutral tone, "The moor must be an ideal place for you to indulge in your passion."

He stilled, cocked an eyebrow. "Oh?"

"All this undisturbed flora and fauna for you to study." I

gave him a bland smile. "Do your family enjoy living out in the wilds, also?"

"Of course."

I caught the flash of a frown pass across Watson's features, then it was gone.

"Yes," Stapleton went on. "I've been here long enough to know these moors like the back of my hand. But I would not advise you to wander too far from the marked trails, if you value your health."

I tried not to bristle. "Meaning?"

Watson turned to point. "My dear, do you see the patches of bright green scattered across this great plain? Stapleton was just telling me that's the Grimpen Mire," He suppressed a shudder. "I've just seen for myself what happens even to large animals which find themselves stuck in it."

"Certain death." Stapleton's pale eyes were fixed on mine for a second. Then they shifted to a point over my shoulder and he darted to the side, unslinging the camera as he went. "Excuse me an instant," he called over his shoulder. "It is another Cyclopides."

Watson and I stood and watched him pursue the butterfly, leaping from tuft to tuft with camera poised.

Not knowing how long he would be occupied, I turned to Watson and said bluntly, "Something about meeting Stapleton's family that worried you, doctor?"

He looked surprised, then shook his head and frowned again. "A misunderstanding, I think, between myself and his sister," he said. "She lives at Merripit House with Stapleton. At first, she mistook me for Sir Henry and was most insistent that I—or, rather, *he*—should leave the moor and never return."

His sister? Ah…

"Did she say why?"

"No. But afterwards she definitely did not want her brother to know she had said such a thing… It was most strange. Perhaps she, too, is worried about strangers becoming engulfed in the Mire."

"Or it could be that living here was more his choice than

hers," I ventured. "And she's giving every newcomer the benefit of her unfortunate experience."

"Indeed. She claimed to be happy, but her voice didn't quite match her words."

And there's a damn good reason for that…

Stapleton was returning, eyes fixed on the view screen on the back of the Nikon as he checked his shots.

"I think I have him that time," he told us, gaze flicking from one to the other. "Ah, yes." He turned the camera around and showed us a sharp close-up of a fairly ordinary looking brown and yellow butterfly. "Really quite beautiful, isn't he?"

The gentleness in his voice almost made me shiver. I left it to Watson to make the right noises.

"I must be getting on, if you'll excuse me, gentlemen?"

"Of course," Watson said. "Oh, just one last thing before you go, Miss Fox. A few minutes before we met, you didn't happen to hear a loud, well, *howling* sound, did you?"

"A howling?" I repeated. "As in a wolf, or a dog?"

"Yes." Watson seemed almost embarrassed to ask. "It was the weirdest, strangest thing I've ever heard in my life."

I shook my head.

"I told you, Dr Watson, I should not be surprised to learn that what we heard was the cry of a bittern," Stapleton said. "At one time they were practically extinct in England, but the population has boomed in recent years."

I had never knowingly heard the sound made by a bittern, but I was not convinced. And if the look on his face was anything to go by, neither was Dr Watson.

———

STAPLETON INVITED me to join the pair of them for lunch at Merripit, but I declined—much, I suspect, to his relief. Instead, I continued on the track leading me towards the holiday cottages, not breaking stride until I was out of their sight.

Then I ducked off the trail and left the rucksack marked by a small pile of stones, turning back without it. I employed every stealth technique I'd ever been taught to cover the ground between me and the Stapletons' without being seen. That telephoto lens of his was a hazard I could have done without. I had no choice but to work around it.

I managed to creep into position nearby, and lay waiting while Watson no doubt enjoyed a pleasant lunch with Jack Stapleton. I'd been told he could be charming company when he set his mind to it.

And downright bloody nasty when he was thwarted.

Watson left Merripit House sooner than I expected and started out in the direction of Baskerville Hall. I debated on going after him, hesitating long enough over the decision for it to be taken out of my hands.

A slim, dark-haired woman slipped out of a doorway at the side of the house and hurried across the moor on an intercept course with the doctor. Knowing I wouldn't reach her beforehand—not without risk of exposing us both—I stayed put.

It wasn't long before I saw her returning, and this time was able to emerge from my hiding place and stop her before she got back to the house. Her stride faltered when she saw me waiting for her by the path, glancing sideways at Merripit as if to satisfy herself that we were not going to be seen.

"Beryl Stapleton?"

I hardly needed her tentative nod of reply. She wore a pair of jeans with a polo-necked sweater, and hugged thin arms around her body, though it was hardly cold.

"When?" she asked.

"As soon as you're ready," I said. "Pack a bag and I'll have you out of here this afternoon."

A cloud passed across her face, stricken with indecision. She glanced behind her again, over towards the house. Or it might have been cast further, in the direction Watson had taken.

"I–I need another day," she said, her voice broken but still with the lilting South American accent of her birthplace. "Two at the most. I—"

She broke off as I stepped forwards, took her wrist and pushed back her sleeve. The bruises on her forearm were livid, and fresh.

"Why, when he does this to you?"

She wrenched her arm loose with more force than it needed. "I cannot explain. I know only that he plans a great wrong, and I must stop him—"

"If you tell me, I'll stop him for you," I said. I thought of Holmes hiding on the moor, and of Watson staying nearby. "Help may be closer to hand than you realise."

"It would be my word against his, and what's the use in that?" she cried. "He has doctors lined up to swear I am incapable of knowing my own mind, that I am delusional. All you will succeed in doing is making him more devious and more cruel than he is already."

I sighed, pulling together a patience I didn't feel. "Beryl, you asked for help to get away from this man. That's why I'm here. Why risk your safety any more than you have to—any more than you have already?"

She hunched down into herself, wouldn't meet my eyes. "Because this is partly my fault," she whispered. "And because it is not only *my* safety that is at stake."

And with that she whirled away and ran back towards the house, her dark hair streaming out behind her like a pennant.

———

"Come in, Mr Holmes," I said, answering a quiet knock on the cottage door. "My turn to cook for you, I think."

I'd spent another soggy day keeping obs on the comings and goings of Merripit House, returning to the cottage tired, wet, cold, and irritable. A hot shower and a change of clothes, though, had improved my mood no end, as did getting the wood-burning stove lit and a stew bubbling away on top in a cast-iron pot.

Sherlock Holmes made himself at home in one of the dining chairs while I dished up the stew into bowls. We ate in companionable silence. It wasn't until he'd set aside his cutlery that the intensity of his gaze turned on me in full.

"Well, Charlie, it would seem that our purposes do indeed intersect."

"Oh?"

"You have been keeping an eye on Sir Henry, I believe."

"Not as such," I said. "I'm keeping an eye on the Stapletons. It just so happens that Sir Henry is spending more and more time there."

"Ah. I allow the distinction." He lifted his coffee mug in salute. "He seems much enamoured of Miss Stapleton, from what I can gather."

"Yes, he does rather, doesn't he? You may want to nip that in the bud."

He made no comment other than to raise one eyebrow. "Is there some reason a wealthy baronet would not make the lady a most suitable husband?"

"None at all…if she weren't already married," I said. "Jack and Beryl Stapleton are not brother and sister—they're husband and wife."

Holmes absorbed this news in silence for a moment. "You have proof?"

"Check the records. He used to run a school somewhere up north. The pair were pictured in the news reports when it closed."

He nodded slowly, spoke almost to himself. "Ah, yes, of course. And no doubt he foresaw that she would be very much more useful to him in the character of a free woman." His gaze turned sharp. "But she has tried to warn off Sir Henry several times—first the note, and then mistaking Watson for Sir Henry here."

"Note?"

"In London, before Sir Henry came down to Devon."

I nodded. "I don't know about that, but I believe Stapleton coerced her into falling in with his plans. He certainly physically and psychologically abuses her."

"And what is your role in this, if you *are* now prepared to tell me?"

"I'm here to get her out."

"So, why haven't you?"

I sighed. "Not for want of trying. I don't do kidnapping. She asked for help and she has to *want* to leave. The arrangements were all in place before I came down here, but since Sir Henry's arrival she's turned...reluctant, shall we say. She believes he's in danger."

"From Stapleton? Indeed, he is," Holmes said, his gaunt face grave in the firelight. "Stapleton is a Baskerville. He knows if he can rid himself of Sir Henry, he's next in line for both title and fortune. I very much doubt he will let the lady—be she wife or sister—stand in his way."

———

I woke in the night and found myself grabbing instinctively for the SIG Sauer, which I'd left covered by a shirt on the chair next to the bed. Heart pounding, I sat upright with senses straining against the darkness for whatever had startled me from sleep.

A second later it came again, the thud of a heavy shoulder to the door of the cottage, followed by muttered curses as the sturdy oak held fast.

I reached towards the lamp, mind flipping through scenarios. Someone was clearly trying to break in. Were they doing so because they knew I was in here? Or because they thought the place was empty?

Could be Jack Stapleton, come to put a stop to his wife's escape plan...

Putting on a light would either warn the intruder I was awake and prepared, or warn him I was here at all. Neither option was bad.

I flicked on the light.

The thudding ceased, then a fist began to bang against the wooden planks more desperately than before. I heard a man's voice, high with alarm, his words incoherent.

Throwing back the duvet, I slid my feet into the boots I'd left by the bedside, and scooped up a flashlight and the pistol. I was otherwise still fully dressed, so it was only a moment before I was by the door, watching the latch jump and rattle with the force of the assault from the outside.

"Back up!" I shouted. "Move away from the door."

"Let me in!" roared the man's voice. It was not one I'd heard before, but so twisted by terror, I'm not sure I would have recognised it anyway. "For the love of *God*, let me in!"

"I'm not opening the door until you move away from it," I shouted back.

The hammering stopped, and I thought he was complying with my order, but the next thing I heard was a muffled cry of fear, then his running footsteps, retreating.

I yanked open the bolt and came out of the cottage in a fast crouch, with the gun extended in my right hand, supported by the flashlight in my left. I caught a glimpse of a bolting figure disappearing between two of the cottages. He ran wildly, arms flailing for balance on the rough ground.

And then, out of the corner of my eye, I saw an animal, big and muscular, streak after him in the light from a clear moon. All I gleaned from that fractional view was an impression of a dark outline moving with speed and aggression, its head and jaws flecked with something like the phosphorescence I'd once seen trailing behind a night ferry.

"What the—?"

I took an involuntary step back. The solid reality of the cottage wall grounded me. I remembered Sir Henry's talk of the family legend that stalked the moor—the hell hound that might very well have frightened his uncle to death.

Squaring my shoulders, I clicked off my flashlight and stepped away from the cottage into a bright patch of moonlight, telling myself firmly that I did not believe in ghosts, and ghouls, and things that went bump in the night.

However, I did believe in the exorcistic powers of twelve 9mm hollow point rounds, and in my ability to place every one of them into the centre of a moving target, even in half-light.

I'd hardly taken half-a-dozen paces when there was a shriek in the middle distance, mingled with the rumbling bellow of a chase hound in full pursuit of prey.

The door to the cottage Sherlock Holmes had been using swung open, and two men burst out, causing me to duck behind the corner of another building, out of sight.

"The hound!" cried Holmes. "Come, Watson! Great heavens, if we are too late!"

The pair ran past my position without pause and were soon swallowed up by the gloom. I considered my options.

Stapleton wished to get rid of Sir Henry Baskerville, that much I knew. If this weird apparition was all part of that plan, then it was not my business. Besides, I'd noted the old army Browning in Watson's hand as he passed. They were at least as well equipped to deal with whatever the strange animal might be.

And there were *two* of them…

———

I ONLY HAD it confirmed who the stranger was a day or so later, when I called in to Grimpen again to pick up my email, and buy milk and bread. I happened to meet Dr Mortimer just leaving his surgery, bag in hand.

"You will no doubt be pleased to hear you need not worry about the escaped prisoner, Selden, any longer, Miss Fox."

"Oh? Has he been captured?" I asked, although it hadn't taken much working out what was the likely fate of the man. Who else might have been loose on the moor?

"In a way," Mortimer replied. "The poor man was no doubt stumbling around in the dark when he seems to have fallen and broken his neck—the night before last, it would be."

"Poor man?" I queried. "If *half* of what he was supposed to have done to his victims was true, it's hard to feel much real sympathy for him."

Mortimer blinked a couple of times. Not the response he'd been expecting, clearly. But I'd never subscribed to the tradition of not speaking ill of the dead.

To cover his confusion, he asked, "And have you otherwise been enjoying your stay so far?"

"I think I'm starting to get to know the moors a little," I said, thinking of the GPS in my rucksack. "How is Sir Henry?"

If anything, Mortimer's frown deepened.

"I am on my way to see him now."

"He's not ill, I trust?"

"Oh no, but he is…concerned. Dr Watson promised to stay

with him until this business was over, and now I understand he has gone back to London on some urgent business, leaving Sir Henry to his own devices."

"Well, I'm sure he will appreciate your company."

"Indeed. Although he has been at Baskerville Hall only a short time, already he has made many friends in the area. The Stapletons have invited him to dine this evening."

I left the doctor climbing into his old BMW and hurried back across the moor path to the cottage. Sure enough, the one Sherlock Holmes had been using was empty, the door locked, and no sign of his occupation visible through the windows.

Had he really gone to London with Watson, and left Sir Henry so vulnerable? Something about that just didn't sit right. I could only hope that his actions were somehow for the sake of the game in which Sherlock Holmes—if Watson's blog was anything to go by—seemed to take such delight.

———

It was not only in the hope of finally convincing Beryl Stapleton to put her escape plan into action that I took up station watching Merripit House as afternoon slid into evening. If Holmes had indeed gone to London with Watson, I felt I owed it to him to keep an eye on his charge while I was here.

The lamps in the house came on, shining like navigation lights across the moor. The Stapletons' housekeeper could be seen bustling in the kitchen, preparing food for their guest, and setting the table in the dining room.

But of Beryl Stapleton, I failed to catch a glimpse.

Even when Sir Henry arrived, and the two men sat down to eat, she didn't put in an appearance. Stapleton had hospitalised her several times in the past, although he'd always managed to talk or threaten her out of pressing charges. For a few moments I wondered if he'd done so again, or even if Holmes had taken my words to heart and had somehow whisked her off to safety in London with him, but dismissed the idea as soon as it formed. To do so would mean abandoning his duty to Sir Henry, and I remained unconvinced that he would act that way, even to rescue an abused spouse.

So, where was she?

I circled the house, staying out of range of the lights. Still, I didn't see her, but I hesitated over going in to find out. Suppose Jack Stapleton had realised what she was planning, had locked her up somewhere, and was now waiting for me to reveal myself?

The soft scrape of boots behind me on the path had me scuttling into cover. Against the darkening sky I could just make out three figures approaching, and my pulse began to pound. So, Stapleton *did* suspect something was amiss, and he'd called in reinforcements.

Then I caught a quiet voice I had come to recognise ask, "Are you armed, Lestrade?"

And a new player, his outline small and wiry, answered, "As long as I have my trousers I have a hip-pocket, and as long as I have my hip-pocket I have something in it."

There were so many ways to take that I didn't know where to start. I smiled in the darkness. So, Holmes had not abandoned his post. It didn't take much guessing to work out the identity of the third member of the group. Where Holmes went, Watson was sure to be alongside him. And who better to have there in the rough stuff than an ex-army medic who'd seen action in Iraq and Afghanistan?

But not everything was going according to plan. It had started out as a clear night, but gradually a mist began to roll across the moor, swamping all before it in a thick impenetrable cloud. The three men moved back towards the higher ground, where their view of the house and the path leading away from it was clearer. I worried, though, that they would be too far away to act in case of trouble.

I used the mist as a shield to creep closer to the house. The kitchen was now in darkness, the door unlocked. I slipped through and up the rear stairs. Just as I reached the landing I heard Stapleton and Sir Henry in the hallway below, and flattened against the panelling.

The two men sounded cordial enough. Stapleton was

expressing doubts that the baronet should drive himself home after the wine and the brandy he'd consumed. Sir Henry said he was happy to leave his car and walk across the moor, although his voice betrayed a certain trepidation.

"In that case, I'll see you on your way," Stapleton said.

Knowing I had little time, I hurried along the upper corridor, trying doors quickly as I passed until I found one that was locked. With no time to consider an alternative, I kicked the panel just inboard of the lock, twice, and heard the screws tear out of the frame.

Inside was a study, the walls covered by blow-up photographs of butterflies and insects. In the centre, tied to one of the beams that supported the roof, was a wide-eyed figure, bound to the pillar with plastic zip-ties and gagged with a towel.

I eased the gag away from her mouth. Beryl's face was swollen, one eye closed to a bloodshot slit. Her clothing was bloodied where she'd been beaten, and had fought against her bindings.

I pulled out a knife, snicked the blade into place and sliced through the tough plastic ties. She all but collapsed onto me.

"Let's get you out of here," I said, biting back my anger. "Right now!"

"No!" Her voice was hoarse, her eyes bright with pain and humiliation. "He plans to kill him—tonight! You *must* save Sir Henry."

"Bollocks. It's you I have to worry about."

"*Please*!" Her eyes overflowed with tears. "Quickly, before it is too late!"

I let out an exasperated sigh. "Holmes and Watson are out there—they'll save Sir Henry."

She sagged with relief, then stiffened again almost at once. "But my husband will get away! There is an old tin mine on an island in the heart of the Mire. That's where he kept the hound, and he has a refuge there. Leave me and go after him, I beg you!"

With a muttered curse, I propped her gently against the base of the beam and whirled away. If that was what she wanted, that was what she was going to get. I ran down the staircase, and out through the still-open front door into the foggy night.

By the time I hit the gravel driveway, the SIG Sauer was in my hand.

I'd spent the last few days carefully going over the moor, logging the paths with the GPS. Stapleton might like to think he knew the only safe ways through the Grimpen Mire, but his methods relied on landmarks and sightlines.

Mine relied on a series of thirty satellites orbiting the planet at a distance of 12,500 miles, and speeds of up to 7,000mph. The receiver I carried would work through glass, plastic, or cloud. Yes, it could be fooled by snow, but it wasn't snowing. The signal could also be delayed by tall buildings, or heavy foliage, but fortunately the moor boasted neither obstacle.

Standard civilian GPS units were accurate to around three metres, but for somewhere like the Grimpen Mire that distance could easily be the difference between life and death. That was why I'd come equipped with a military-grade receiver which was accurate to less than 300mm.

I used it now as I jogged into the territory of the Mire, trying to trust in the technology and to avoid listening to the sucking of the bog at the soles of my boots.

Suddenly, over to my right came a cry of outright fear, and the same roaring growl I'd heard the night that Selden had been run to his death.

I froze. There was a pause, then gunshots, their sharp report muffled by the fog, followed by a yelp of pain that I could hardly tell if it was human or animal in origin.

The GPS guided me on. I kept one eye on the screen and the other scanning the landscape ahead of me, as far as I could see into it for the fog. After another fifty metres or so I began to imagine it might be thinning. Then I knew for certain that it was, as the figure of a man sprawled on his back solidified ahead of me.

"Help!"

As I approached I saw it was Jack Stapleton. He'd stepped off the safe path and the Mire had grabbed him as far as his knees in a heartbeat. But he possessed a coolly logical brain and was not a man to panic easily. He'd taken the recommended action, lying down flat with his arms outstretched to spread his weight across the surface, which was not stopping him sinking farther, but was at least slowing his rate of descent. With his legs encased to the knees, he could not extricate himself unaided. He daren't even lift his head at my arrival, and only his eyes swivelled to meet mine.

"Ah… Miss Fox. Thank God," he began. "I don't have much time. I—"

And then he saw the 9mm in my right hand. His mouth worked soundlessly for a second, and I watched his mind considering whether to admit defeat or try to brazen it out.

"Well, well," he said at last. "I didn't think Sir Henry would call on the services of another—not when he had the great Sherlock Holmes at his disposal."

"I'm not working for Sir Henry," I said. "I'm actually working for Señora Maria Pablo de Silva Garcia."

"Who?"

"Oh, you really should recognise the name, Jack. She's your mother-in-law. A very formidable lady, who does not appreciate the way you've treated her daughter."

I squatted down, as close as I was prepared to get to either Stapleton or the bog that had him in its grip.

He bared his teeth at me. "So what are you waiting for." His eyes flicked to the gun. "Just get it over with, why don't you?"

I shook my head. "Not my brief to kill you, Jack."

I watched the play of emotions cross his face then. Doubt, chased by logic into hope, and relief. "So, give me your hand then. Get me out of here."

I shook my head again, rising to my feet. "Sorry, Jack," I said without regret. "Not my brief to save you, either."

"I'll admit everything!" he cried. "About Sir Charles, about the hound. About—"

I smiled. "Do you really think 'the great Sherlock Holmes' hasn't worked it all out for himself?" I asked. "The only thing he needed was the proof. And I think you've provided him with plenty tonight. That, and Beryl's testimony."

"She can have the divorce uncontested! I won't fight her on anything."

"Too late, Jack." I looked at him, cold-eyed as the mud

sucked at his clothing, plucked at his hair. "Ask yourself which is worse—the long, slow death of drowning? Or the even longer, even *slower*, death of life behind bars?"

He was still for a moment longer, then he began to thrash, grunting with effort. His actions agitated the Mire beneath him, so that it drew him under ever more quickly. After less than a minute he'd driven himself below the surface, which continued to bubble and heave for a while, then returned to malignant stasis.

I slid the 9mm back into its rig and glanced at the screen of the GPS, stepping carefully onto the patches of solid ground in the direction of the cottage.

The sky was beginning to lighten, and a breeze had sprung up to disperse the remaining fog. I reckoned I'd just time to pack my gear and walk to the station in time to catch the London train. Beryl would be safe in the hands of Dr Watson and Dr Mortimer.

And not even Sherlock Holmes would be able to say, with any certainty, what fate had befallen Jack Stapleton.

———

More to Read!

If you liked this, then you may also like the later Charlie Fox novels, where she is in full-blown professional bodyguard mode. Why not take a look at CHARLIE FOX: BODYGUARD eBoxset of books 4, 5, and 6? And please check out the rest of the series **here**, including FOURTH DAY, which sees Charlie on another rescue mission—this time inside a secretive California cult.

AFTERWORD

Liked it?

If you've enjoyed this collection of stories, there is no greater compliment you can give the author than to leave a brief, honest and heartfelt review on the retailer site where you made your purchase, on goodreads, or social media. Doesn't have to be long or in great detail, but it means a huge amount if you'd write a few words to say what you thought about it, and encourage others to give my work a try. Thank you so much for taking the time.

I'm only human…

We all make mistakes from time to time. This collection has gone through numerous editing, copyediting, and proofreading stages before making it out into the world. Still, occasionally errors do creep past us. If by any chance you do spot a blooper, please let me, the author, know about it. That way I can get the error corrected as soon as possible. Plus I'll send you a free digital edition of one of my other short stories as a thank you for your eagle-eyed observational skills! Email me at **Zoe@ZoeSharp.com**.

Please Note

This book was written in British English and UK spellings and punctuation have been used throughout.

ABOUT THE AUTHOR

Zoë Sharp opted out of mainstream education at the age of twelve and wrote her first novel at fifteen. She created her award-winning crime thriller series featuring ex-Special Forces trainee turned bodyguard, **Charlotte 'Charlie' Fox**, after receiving death threats in the course of her work as a photojournalist. She has been making a living from her writing since 1988, and since 2001 has written various novels: the highly acclaimed Charlie Fox series, including a prequel novella; standalone crime thrillers; and collaborations with espionage thriller author John Lawton, as well as numerous short stories. Her work has been used in Danish school textbooks, inspired an original song and music video, and been optioned for TV and film.

For Behind the Scenes, Bonus Features, Freebies, Sneak Peeks and advance notice of new stories, sign up for Zoë's **VIP list** at **www.ZoeSharp.com/vip-mailing-list**.

Zoë is always happy to hear from readers, reader groups, libraries or bookstores. You can contact her at **Zoe@ZoeSharp.com**

Visit Zoë's Amazon Author Page

facebook.com/ZoeSharpAuthor

twitter.com/authorzoesharp

goodreads.com/authorzoesharp

amazon.com/author/zoesharp

instagram.com/authorzoesharp

THE STORIES SO FAR...

FOURTH DAY #8: A man joins the Fourth Day cult to prove they killed his son. By the time Charlie and Sean get him out, he's convinced otherwise. Then he dies...

FIFTH VICTIM #9: How can Charlie protect the daughter of a rich Long Island banker when the girl seems determined to put them both in harm's way?

DIE EASY #10: A deadly hostage situation in New Orleans forces Charlie to improvise as never before. And this time she can't rely on Sean to watch her back.

ABSENCE OF LIGHT #11: In the aftermath of an earthquake, Charlie's working alongside a team who dig out the living and ID the dead, and hoping they won't find out why she's *really* there.

FOX HUNTER #12: Charlie can never forget the men who put a brutal end to her army career, but she swore a long time ago she would never go looking for them. Now she doesn't have a choice.

BAD TURN #13: Charlie is out of work, out of her apartment and out of options. Why else would she be working for a shady arms dealer?

TRIAL UNDER FIRE # prequel: The untold story. Before she was a bodyguard, she was a soldier...

FOX FIVE RELOADED: short story collection. Charlie Fox. In small bites. With sharp teeth.

Where to Start?

If you enjoy reading about Charlie Fox right in the thick of it, working in close protection and travelling all over the world, I'd recommend you start with **FIRST DROP: #4**, or **CHARLIE FOX: BODYGUARD eBoxset #2**.

If, however, you want the full story of what happened to Charlie after she left the Army, and how she found her way into close protection, you'll want to start at the beginning, with **KILLER INSTINCT: #1**, or **CHARLIE FOX: THE EARLY YEARS eBoxset #1**.

the CSI Grace McColl and Detective Nick Weston Lakes crime thrillers

DANCING ON THE GRAVE: #1 A sniper with a mission, a CSI with something to prove, a young cop with nothing to lose, and a teenage girl with a terrifying obsession. The calm of the English Lake District is about to be shattered.

BONES IN THE RIVER: #2 Driving on a country road, late at night, you hit a child. There are no witnesses. You have *everything* to lose. What do you do?

standalone crime thrillers

THE BLOOD WHISPERER Six years ago CSI Kelly Jacks woke next to a butchered body with the knife in her hands and no memory of what happened. She trusted the evidence would prove her innocent. It didn't. Is history now repeating itself?

AN ITALIAN JOB (with **John Lawton**) Former soldiers Gina and Jack are about to discover that love is far deadlier the second time around.

*the **Blake & Byron** mystery thrillers*

THE LAST TIME SHE DIED She came back on the day of her father's funeral, ten years after she vanished. But she can't be who she says she is. Because we killed her. Didn't we?

Made in United States
Cleveland, OH
29 December 2024